Misfit

Misfit

a novel

Adam Braver

TIN HOUSE BOOKS / Portland, Oregon & New York, New York

Published by Tin House Books, Portland, Oregon, and New York, New York
Distributed to the trade by Publishers Group West, 1700 Fourth St., Berkeley, CA 94710, www.pgw.com

Library of Congress Cataloging-in-Publication Data

Braver, Adam, 1963-
 Misfit : a novel / Adam Braver. — 1st U.S. ed.
    p. cm.
 ISBN 978-1-935639-40-4 (trade paper) — ISBN 978-1-935639-41-1 (ebook)
 1. Monroe, Marilyn, 1926-1962—Fiction. 2. Motion picture actors and actresses—Fiction. I. Title.
 PS3602.R39M57 2012
 813'.6--dc23

Chapters from this book originally appeared in the following publications: "On the Day of Her Wedding" in the *Normal School*; "Dressing Marilyn Monroe" in the *Pinch*; and "Norwalk State Hospital" in *New South*.

First U.S. edition 2012

Printed in the USA

Interior design by Janet Parker
www.tinhouse.com

For Mel

1961–2010

Also by Adam Braver

Mr. Lincoln's Wars
Divine Sarah
Crows Over the Wheatfield
November 22, 1963

July 27, 1962
———————————

Marilyn Monroe's House, Los Angeles

9:15 AM

She's going to Lake Tahoe to get away for the weekend. It's that simple.

Sitting in the living room, one hand gripped around the handle of her suitcase and the other on her make-up case, she waits to be picked up and driven to the air-field. The room is sparse, with a small leather cocktail table, a long Italian bench that serves as a couch, and a hearth screen covering the never-used fireplace. The only other furnishings are two folding benches, which, in the dim room, look bony and ordinary, caged by the bars of sunlight streaking around the curtains. Nevertheless, the wood floors gleam—her housekeeper, Eunice, waxed them earlier, then moved on to the master bedroom, where she's making the bed. When she's finished, Eunice will gather the dirty glasses and dishes to wash in the kitchen; before leaving, she'll crack open the bedroom window, enough to let in some fresh air.

She's impatient for this weekend to get under way. When Frank invited her to the Cal Neva Lodge, his hotel on the lake, he said, *Sometimes you need to get away*, and there was no argument there. He promised to look out for her. Keep her protected from those industry clowns who are suing her and hassling her over her latest movie. Frank will watch out for her with no strings; he's probably the only person on earth whom she can trust to provide her with such a sanctuary. No press. No studio. No concerns. Just her usual cabin. And the lake, which always brings her peace.

Quickly, for assurance, she inventories everything Eunice helped her pack—from her clothes to her cosmetics to her pills. But before she can get through her mental checklist, she considers what's not being taken, what's being left behind. Almost nothing. She's hardly furnished the house; what little furniture she's bought (mostly in Mexico) is stored on pallets, still wrapped in shipping plastic. And each room has been appointed with only the bare minimum, just enough to be functional. She imagines seeing the house from a field anthropologist's perspective, moving among the few artifacts to understand how a life was lived, and finding nothing but shards that support vague assumptions of a shifting culture.

Checking her watch, she stands up and walks to the window. She parts the curtains and peers down the driveway. The bright green shrubs and the sun-soaked palms make the living room seem even darker. And that much more empty. She can't wait to get out.

She calls down the hall to Eunice, asking if she knows when the car is scheduled to come. "Wasn't it supposed to be here by now?"

Eunice answers, "It should be arriving any minute." Her voice echoes, along with the rattling dishes she's carrying into the kitchen. "We have to give the driver some breathing room at this hour."

"That's what worries me. It might take forever to get to the airport. I don't trust the traffic on Sepulveda this time of day."

Eunice steps out of the kitchen, staying at the end of the hallway. She has her cat-eye glasses off and wipes the lenses with her apron. "It's a private plane," she says. "Mr. Sinatra won't let it leave without you."

"I know," she says, her voice sounding tinny. "I know. It's just that . . ."

Eunice tells her it will be okay. There is no need to worry. She puts her glasses back on; they gleam brightly in the dark corridor. Then Eunice heads back to the kitchen, repeating that there is no need to worry. Her tone is oddly definitive.

She's anxious to get to Lake Tahoe, away from all the dramas and the systems that reinforce her being Marilyn Monroe. Anxious to get into the cabin and let her troubles evaporate over the lake. She knows how to disappear for a while. She's been doing it her whole life. But the timing has to be right. There are certain forces that will line up, waiting to collide. And when you sense they're coming, and you're ready to jump, it's critical that you're in that exact space the moment just before the collision, like being present for your own private big bang theory.

But it's not that complicated. In fact, it's kind of simple.

1937–1954

As a little girl in church, she had to pin her hands under her
thighs to keep from taking off her clothes. It was an urge
she consciously had to fight. It even came to her in dreams.
Atonement? Vengeance? Vulnerability? Or maybe the need to be
seen as she really was.

In an FBI report about Marilyn Monroe, dated March
6, 1962, it's noted that the subject "feels like a 'negated sex
symbol.'"

1937: Ida Martin's House, Compton, CA

And the best place for it is just above your bed, but the walls are bare, and there are no marks on them, not even pinholes, and you don't want to ask because you don't want to bring anything up, this being your first day here and all, although you do get the feeling that you'll never want to bring anything up, no matter how many days pass. So you take the copy of *Time* with Clark Gable on the cover and stick it under the lining in your suitcase, where it always will be whenever you want to see it. You've had the issue for nearly a year already, carrying it between addresses. It was a gift from the Goddards' neighbors after they said they'd read it and too many newer issues were piling up by the week. You couldn't imagine how anybody would part with something so special. It makes you feel safe to know he's always there. Head cocked and looking right at you with a slightly concerned smile.

You've been back and forth between your mother's house and the Bolender foster home since you were born, and then the Goddards in Van Nuys, and then to the Los Angeles Orphans Home, and back to the Goddards, and now here. And you're only eleven! But this should be a better situation. In Compton. Not far from Hawthorne, where you lived longest. But a little far from Norwalk, and your mother's hospital, which might have its plusses, as she won't be able to just show up and maybe do something to humiliate you. And at least you're with family: Mrs. Martin, her daughter, Olive, and Olive's children. When you were first informed you'd be going to live with Mrs. Martin and her family, everybody referred to your great-aunt as Aunt Ida. But when you walked into the bungalow, and she was standing there, firm in stance, with the crucifix on the wall looking like it could ghost forward all on its own to hang right over her head in thin air, you realized she would never be Aunt Ida but always Mrs. Martin. And though she'll insist on you addressing her as Aunt Ida, and you'll force it out of your mouth, your head will always keep saying Mrs. Martin.

At the orphans' home you lived under a set of rules. Here you feel as though you live under a single rule: the Bible. As with all the other homes, being in your bedroom with your few belongings is manageable, the one place you have a sense of solitude. But the moment you step out into the house, you turn light-headed and forgetful and must appear to be feebleminded. The goal is always to get through the chores and meals and duties, and then scamper back to your room, where you can dig out that *Time* cover. Stare into it, believing it's a portal into something better.

You're on the edge of his bed. Your cousin Buddy invited you to hang out in his room, as though it were some kind of honor. You've been trying to avoid him since you got here. Maybe because he seemed too welcoming, and one thing you've learned after so much shuffling around is not to trust the people who are too welcoming. Especially the boys. But his invitation is presented as something special: he can now trust you being in his home. His talk is clever, and after a sentence or two he makes you feel you've earned his attention, and you get a sudden swell of pride. For just a moment you forget that you never wanted to be around him in the first place. Even though he's a teenager, Buddy's dressed in the clothes his grandmother lays out for him—khaki pants and a button-down white shirt. Always ironed. You're in a dress, one that reaches past your ankles. Mrs. Martin says the only use for any other hemline is to tempt the devil. Although you're not convinced the devil wouldn't, Buddy will never go in your room. It's for a child. Too spare and unworldly.

His is for a young man. Still, it smells of boy, a stale, salty stink, so thick that even an open window can't clear it out. Initially, his room looks clean. Mrs. Martin wouldn't have it any other way. And several times a day she passes by, looking in through the cracked door, commenting that cleanliness is next to godliness. But from your vantage point on the bed, the little messes begin to reveal themselves. A pile of dirty socks. Balls of dust. Crumpled pages. They're in the corners, where no one ever looks.

"Don't be scared," he says. "I told you you're welcome here."

"I'm not scared." What else could you possibly say?

"Oh, I bet you have a touch of your mama's nerves in you."

"I'm not scared," you repeat with a whisper, staring straight at the crack in the door. Maybe Mrs. Martin will come by for one more look.

"Don't you worry," he says. "This is a normal house. My grandmother makes sure we're protected by God." He reaches over and squeezes your shoulder. For a moment, you have the feeling he has the strength to lift the bone straight out.

"We're normal too," you say.

"You're going to have to speak up. I can barely hear you."

"We've just hit a streak is all, me and my mother. A streak." You shrug your shoulder with a little jolt, but his hand doesn't move.

He says, "A *streak*," and laughs in a kind of annoying way. Slightly pious. And mostly mean. "Well there's no streaks here," he says. "We're all even-steven."

"I'll be going home soon enough. Once my mother's able to return to work." You scoot a little closer to the edge of the bed. Part of you hopes you'll just tumble off. "She works in Hollywood, you know. On the pictures."

He moves in closer.

"She cuts films. Edits them. But she knows lots of movie stars. Been right in the thick of it. So we're going to be fine."

His hand moves from your shoulder and slopes down your front; only the cotton of your dress separates his palm from your skin. Your chest has just begun to form, and you've barely put your hands there yourself. It hasn't yet seemed like your body. But his hands are there. Without thought. And at first it's as though you're watching it, like you're floating up above, but then you start to feel forced, locked down, and you get real cold, like a sheet of ice is making a glacier over your skin, yet you're burning up so much inside that before it can form, the ice melts into a thick stream of cool sweat; and your stomach is tumbling and churning and you're afraid you might throw up at any second. But creepiest of all, and what makes this have almost no sense whatsoever, is how sincere Buddy looks, as though there's not a creepy bone in his body, only charity. And when his hands slide down over your belly, all you can think about is how you just want to be home, but you can't picture any one place as home, and so you try to inch yourself away, just bit by bit, until there's no more bed, and you could just tumble off.

On Sunday Mrs. Martin dresses you, and you no longer look eleven, but instead like a smaller version of an old churchwoman, with no shape or form or sex. Stockings up to your thighs. Black shoes too heavy to walk in. The outfit is appropriate because church is where she's taking you. She says you need it. She doesn't like how withdrawn you've been the past couple of days. (You suspect that's a veiled remark about your mother more than any inkling that something horrible has happened under her roof.) Then she amends her statement to say we all need it. It's our only path to goodness. (So maybe she does have an inkling.) You ask if Buddy is going, and she mutters he's not, he's had a conflict with his mother's schedule, and you don't ask what, and she doesn't bother to explain, and you're relieved because you know that if he came you'd be forced to sit next to him in the pews.

You know you ought to tell her. Tell her the truth about what Buddy did. But you don't know how. And you wonder if she knows by the way she acts as though she doesn't.

Sitting beside you in the pew, she leans over and barks in a sharp whisper that you should cross your legs. "Send the invitation," she says, "and you'll get the RSVPs." And she directs you to lower your head when you smile. And when walking through a crowded area keep your gaze focused on either the ground at your feet or an object in front of you. Eye contact can send the improper message. She says not to be fooled just because this is a church. Temptation is everywhere, and it thrives on testing, and what better place to test temptation than in a house of worship. When you look up at her and nod, indicating you understand, she slaps the back of her hand against your knee. Her jaw is clenched. "Didn't I just tell you to keep your head down?"

The preacher stands before the congregation, and he howls out the word *salvation*. He lets it just hang there; he won't talk again until the word has faded from the sanctuary. He is small, and he is slight, but he looks a million feet tall, rising through his tan coat into the rafters, high above, while his blue tie points down at the floor. "Salvation," he finally says, "is the only chance we've got." He's got a bellowing voice. And he paces back and forth, floating side to side. But no matter where he is, his voice seems aimed right at you. And you take it all inside you. "We all need to think about how we can correct for the missteps we take. And how do you know when you misstep? Because your feet get weary. Tired. And they start to burn, and we all know that burning that you're feeling is coming from below. That's right. Every misstep you take is a step closer to the devil. And the only thing that can pull you back?

Salvation. It's right there in Psalms 24: 4–5: *He that hath clean hands, and a pure heart; who hath not lifted up his soul unto vanity, nor sworn deceitfully. He shall receive the blessing from the Lord, and righteousness from the God of his salvation.* Or as our friends in Acts tell us, *To open their eyes, and to turn them from darkness to light, and from the power of Satan unto God, that they may receive forgiveness of sins, and inheritance among them which are sanctified by faith that is in me.*" And you feel your body tingling. He knows just what you're thinking, but also how you can be freed. And you have the strange compulsion to slip out of the costume Mrs. Martin has dressed you in and just sit there naked, letting all this possibility wash over you, and, in a way, kind of love you. "There's only but one place for you to go for eternal salvation, and you're all going to have to walk right through those gates on your own. But you will not be able to do it with the devil burning at your feet, and so you all are going to have to trust me on this—there is no one who can wash your feet but yourself. And that's a fact."

Filing out of the church, you feel inspired. Finally there is a sense of right that you understand, and there is muscle behind it to back you up. The preacher is standing by the doors, shaking hands with the congregants. It's bright outdoors. But the sunlight stops at the doorway, not spilling into the nave, where the only light is a sparkle from a stained-glass window, making diamonds on the dark wood. The preacher takes

your great-aunt's hand.
Martin," he says.

She responds, "Such

"And who do we hav‹

She introduces you. ⸝
you're staying with her o⸱
while, only until the motł
not clear if her emphasis on   ⸱⸱⸱use
there is something about you ⸱⸱ ⸱⸱e finds embarrass-
ing, or if she's underscoring her sense of charity. The
preacher takes your hand as a welcome. And a blush
comes on so warm and fierce you can feel it boring
down into your toes. It's as though he's spotted your
desire to be naked, and even saw you as such, maybe
X-rayed you with the power that he has. All you can
do (and remembering what Mrs. Martin said earlier) is
look down.

Mrs. Martin smiles at the preacher, and she puts
her hand on your shoulder, squeezing in the exact spot
where Buddy did earlier in the week. She's talking to
you but looking right at the preacher. "Don't you have
something you want to say, my dear?"

You flounder for words. Search as though language
is something new, while they both wait. She squeezes
again, and, like a reflex, the words push out: "Thank
you."

"I'll pray for your mother," he says, "but I'll expect you to take the reins of your own life, honestly
and truly . . . Remember, the power of God will guide

ong as you live righteously." And then he turns
our great-aunt. "And bless you, Mrs. Martin. Keep
spreading the word, and living by it."

"Amen," she says. "Amen."

The ride home is silent. You look out the window
at the orchards going by, rehearsing how you're going
to tell her about Buddy. You'll do it right when you get
home, while Buddy and his mother are still gone, and
Mrs. Martin is at her most pious. Your mouth goes a
little dry thinking about it. Your head a little foggy. But
you have the power of God behind you. And you're
obliged to have clean hands and a clear heart.

First she slaps you across the face. Then she tells you
you're disgusting. And she says she will tolerate no
such talk in her house. She says maybe you talk that
way with your mother, but not in this house. You
stand there in the living room, face tingling and on
fire. She paces around you, hands opening and closing,
and you can hear her breath as though you're deep
inside her lungs. Then she stomps into the kitchen,
but comes right out. Circles you. Three times around.
You're almost too dizzy to stand, but too light to fall.
And you do everything within your power to make
yourself invisible (clench your fists, squeeze your eyes,
summon all your will), but when you glance down you
still see your hand sticking out of the cuff of the dress
she put you in. And then she disappears to her bedroom. And you're alone in the living room (maybe the

first time you've been alone anywhere in this house other than your room?). For a moment your shoulders drop. Your head clears. And you draw in a breath, inflating some life back into yourself. It will be okay. The shock has passed. You tell yourself that over and over again. But then you hear her footsteps coming out of the bedroom. And they're not just squeaking the hardwoods; they sound as though they're breaking them. You shoot your eyes to the floor. Don't dare glance up. Hope she'll only pass on through. But again she circles. Round and round. And then she stops behind you. She's mumbling. Over and over. An incantation. And at first the words make no sense. But as she keeps repeating them, you pick up the rhythm, and you start to find the words, *For if ye forgive men their trespasses, your heavenly Father will also forgive you . . . For if ye forgive men their trespasses, your heavenly Father will also forgive you . . . For if ye forgive men their trespasses, your heavenly Father will also forgive you . . . For if ye forgive men their trespasses, your heavenly Father will also forgive you . . .* Soon you're chanting it over and over in your head, as though it's the only sound in the entire universe, with the words becoming almost nonsensical. The first blow drops you to your knees. Across the back and between the shoulder blades. It's something hard, like a cane, whistling by your ear when she pulls it back. And you brace. Prepare for another blow. You want to say *no*. You want to say anything. But you have no voice. There are no words inside you. *For if ye forgive men their trespasses, your heavenly Father will also forgive you . . . For if ye forgive men their trespasses, your heavenly Father will also forgive you . . . For if ye forgive men their trespasses, your heavenly Father will also forgive you . . .* She doesn't stop. Even for a breath. And then it smacks down on you again. But you don't fall off your knees until the fourth blow. And as you lie on the floor, being beaten from the back of your thighs up to your shoulders and back down your rear, all you can think of is crawling away, climbing into your suitcase, somehow magically snapping the latches and locking yourself inside, holding on to Clark Gable, both of you stowing away into another life where this one will become nothing more than a pitiable story.

1945: Metropolitan Airport, Van Nuys, CA

In the old Timm Aircraft plant at Metropolitan Airport, movie actor Reginald Denny set up a manufacturing shop. In the early thirties, his acting career in full bloom, Denny, a former RAF pilot in World War I, opened a model-plane store on Hollywood Boulevard, initially calling it Reginald Denny Enterprises but soon recasting it as the Radioplane Company. The crown jewel was the remote-controlled plane that he and his team developed: the Dennymite. Initially built in 1938 with the hobbyist in mind, Denny's plane garnered interest from the army. A radio-controlled model airplane would be perfect for training antiaircraft artillerymen. Now he produces the OQ-2 drones. Daily, by the hundreds. Located in Van Nuys, about twenty miles outside of Los Angeles, Metropolitan Airport is an industrial center surrounded by farmland. Once the airport to the stars, and later auxiliary soundstages for the pictures, the airport was bought in 1942 by the military, which then converted many of the buildings into manufacturing centers for defense while still maintaining the soundstages. At one end, aircraft was being assembled; at the other, scenes from *Casablanca* were being filmed. Now, in the midforties, production is in full swing. The civilian workers, mostly women, are dedicated, faceless in our anonymity, with a posture that conveys a sense of pride in its stoutness. We build the drones. Measure the balsa. Cut. Assemble and glue. Some paint the parts. Stretch fabric over the frame. Others make miniature parachutes, which, down the line, are folded inside the fuselage. Some of us inspect for quality control.

We're all orphans in here. Seated at tables along the perimeter of this giant warehouse, forming the production line. It's a home for girls. It's an income. And it supports the war effort. But more than anything it's something to do. Something to keep your mind off being a bride who has lost her footing since her husband was shipped away. All of us may be alone, but at least we're alone together. Most of the time we're all thinking the same things, and carrying the same worries, and while at times it can feel good to say them out loud as some kind of verification or reminder that you're not alone with these feelings, the truth is that most of the time giving voice to any of your thoughts usually makes you feel more alone. Like you wish you'd never said anything. There are a lot of us girls in here, but it still feels hollow and distant, maybe on account of us being in a hangar, where the ceiling lifts high above us and the metal beams are crisscrossed, exposed, and the reminder of the room's true function only makes you feel smaller, and lesser, and fewer.

She always sits in the same places, be it her workstation or the same chair in the break room for lunch, and it's hard to tell if it's out of habit, insolence, or indifference. She would blend with all the others if it weren't for her seeming dedication to not being noticed and heard. The rest of us girls are always carrying on, fighting for attention with our stories, and worries, and gossip. She carries herself best with the older women, the ones whose husbands left career jobs to go fight, who seem as though they've seen it all before and have lost the energy to fight to establish any presence. But a sadness coats her face as a kind of dull foundation. She can't be more than nineteen; her face looks like it's still forming, her shoulders slim and fragile, her body only recently burst, and when she talks it's easy to forget what she's saying; instead you study her face, trying to see what she'll look like when she's old, and the funny thing is that it's impossible to tell, like trying to imagine the finish cracking on smooth porcelain. She gives off the feeling of someone who's lived this life before. Knows what it's like to be in a world of displaced women. And how it's navigated. It's the mechanicalness of the work that soothes her, she says. And sometimes we can catch a glimpse of her, staring straight across the hangar, her hands stretching and tightening a parachute's fabric before she glances down to inspect it, and we can see what she's envisioning: a room all cozy and yellow-lighted from a setting sun; she sits on a dark brown couch in front of a fireplace, a book on her lap, and a nerve up her back so calm and at ease that she wouldn't even flinch if the book dropped off her lap and slammed on the floor.

She'll answer questions, but she doesn't say much about herself. Her husband of a couple years left his job at Lockheed a year ago, driven by his calling for the uniform. He enlisted as a merchant marine, first working as a physical fitness instructor and then deployed to the South Pacific by ship when the war began. His being a merchant marine initially gave her some sense of ease. After all, their role is just to transport troops and supplies. And she says that so naively, as though he's not actually moving through a war zone in the South Pacific. "Isn't it basically the navy?" a gal to the left says to her, but she shakes her head and repeats, "It's the merchant marines," and she doesn't say it with any sense of pride, just as a matter of fact. We never intend to be cruel in here, just practical, because it seems that a practical outlook will make whatever might happen easier to bear. We've seen it before. We know how it works. A girl on her right says, "Wouldn't the Japs go after his ship just the same as they would any other?" "Especially," another interjects, "if it's carrying supplies. They'd want to cut it off. I imagine it would be the first target. It's what they do with lifelines." Again, we're not trying to be cruel. Only being practical. But she's not listening. She's drifting away, while her hands stay at work. Eyes sailing away from us. Going off into that room of hers.

Sometimes she puts on like she really misses him. Other times it's hard to tell. One time she said she was fed to him. We never knew what she meant, *fed*. A couple of us local to Van Nuys knew his name; he was a big football star in high school. But that's about all we knew. Another time she told a story about a camping trip up in the mountains at Big Bear, and she told it like it was one of those things she really missed—we've all got our own, the one memory that really sums up how much we miss our husbands—but after she told it, and her eyes were all watery, some of us swore she told it like she was never there. Like the way people try to place themselves inside a magazine ad or movie, wishing it were their life.

Once, she said she'd had a miscarriage just before he left. Another time, she said she wished they'd tried to get pregnant, so they would've at least had their life in motion when he returned. She talks with such sincerity. Even when her stories don't always match.

She says that after work, when she gets home to her mother-in-law's house, supper is always waiting for her, and they sit on the couch, eating, looking at two photos of him; one is his senior portrait and the other is a military portrait. They just sit there quietly, and neither of them bothers to make conversation. Like a cross between watching a movie and visiting a grave site. We ask if she ever goes to her own folks' house. She replies with an authority in her voice we've never heard before (or at least never noticed): her mama's often occupied and her daddy's an important man in the movies. We ask who he is. Do we know him? And she raises a funny little smile, almost impish, and says, "Now, ladies, if I told you who he is, then you'd never treat me the same again."

Ronald Reagan, now *Captain* Ronald Reagan, is assigned to the army air force's First Motion Picture Unit in Culver City. He produces training films for the army air force. One of his duties is to build enthusiasm for the war effort through promoting the solidarity of sacrifice among those back home. The war is everybody's responsibility. In a sense, we're all soldiers. To this end, Captain Reagan wants stories of ordinary Americans hard at work. Reginald Denny, his old acting friend, suggests the Radioplane Company, where pretty young girls stretch canvas over miniature airplane fuselages. Dainty and ordinary, yet just as committed as their brothers and boyfriends and husbands and fathers stationed in Europe. That kind of story is sure to raise morale. And so Captain Reagan arranges for a spread in *Yank* magazine. And when the army photographer, a young private, shows up for the shoot at midmorning, we're all sitting just a little bit straighter, patting our hair down, and rolling on an extra layer of lipstick.

Except for her.

She doesn't fuss. There is nothing out of the ordinary in her behavior. In fact, she barely even looks up when the private walks through, squinting while he sets up the shot in his head, squatting and taking in all the different angles. While we sway right to left with each of the private's movements like stalks in the breeze, she just keeps her hands on task, today screwing propellers onto the little bodies.

We've never thought of her as pretty. Not striking in any standout way. Her face is sweet and her smile is warm enough. But she's not someone you'd pick out of a crowd. Or even remember from one day to the next.

The private says we should just ignore him, pretend he's not here. Act natural. Then he proceeds to move up and down the production line, taking pictures of us from various angles. We're not supposed to pose, but we do find ways to lift our chins, or turn in slight profile, and even sneak in a tempting expression.

Those of us farther down the line glance out of the corners of our eyes, seeing how far away he is, rehearsing our poses in our heads. But she just continues to work. Never looking up. Just one more propeller on one more fuselage.

Then something curious happens. The private snaps a photo of her. And then he snaps another. Not only does he stop moving down the line, it's as though he's been walled off. He drops his bag to the floor and kicks it forward; his legs go into a horseback-riding stance, and he brings the camera up to his face with both hands and starts clicking. One picture after the next.

And she still doesn't look up. It's hard to say if she's that oblivious, or if she's that natural. But he doesn't stop.

Finally, after what seems long enough, he puts down the camera. We all begin our mental rehearsals again. He walks up to her, trying to talk in a hushed voice, but it's just noisy enough in this hangar that everybody has to talk loudly to be heard, and therefore we can always hear every conversation. He tells her he has some ideas for a different kind of photo. He says he can't get over how comfortable she is in front of the camera. And then he asks if she has a sweater, and she says she does, and he says to get it, but she says she's on her shift, and he says what about during lunch, that should be soon, and she keeps screwing on the propellers, head down, lifting her eyes only when she talks, and she says she supposes that would be okay, if he thinks it's best. And he says great, and steps backward, nearly tripping over his bag, and in that moment we have to wonder if we haven't all been had.

She returns to her seat after lunch. Still wearing the sweater. She called him Shutterbug when he left, and she said *sure*, and we didn't know what *sure* meant, until he said he'd be certain to get more film and then take care of finding the location. But what is most striking, or perhaps most memorable, is how different she looks since she's returned. It's like her bones have settled into something more solid. Her walk is poised. The men who work here stop and take notice like something around her is all sexed up. The little girl has gone out of her face, leaving a womanly confidence that is at once stunning, alluring, and a little frightening. And when she sits, it seems as though she's still standing. As if she's grown a little larger. There's never a moment when she acts as though she's no longer one of us, but we get the feeling that she's no longer one of us.

But oddest of all is how we can't keep from staring at her.

You wouldn't know she'd ever had a husband. Since that day she modeled for the private, she never talks about him anymore. Never gives an update. Nothing about the merchant marines, or her opinion about the war. It's not as though her fidelity is in question. It's more like you get the feeling that she never was married. Never part of a family or anything else. Just materialized. As though she's existed out of nowhere.

She tells us she's been posing for the private regularly, and that one weekend he drove her out to the Mojave Desert for a session. And he told her she's a natural, and apparently he's even managed to get some interest in her portfolio, and there's talk of some money for a specific job, and the private predicts that once the *Yank* spread runs she can leave this lousy job. And then she pauses. Stares down at the floor, then looks up, slowly scanning all our faces. For a moment she looks like her old self. "I didn't mean *lousy*," she says. "It's just an expression. You know that." After she spits that out, her posture straightens, and she's back to her new self. We tell her it's okay. But what we don't say is that we know she did mean *lousy*. We know exactly what she meant.

And one of the girls says to her, "What does your husband think?" And she says, "What?" and we're not sure if her *what* refers to whether she has a husband or whether she has a thing for him to think about. "About the pictures? About all the modeling you've been doing while he's gone." "I don't worry him with those kinds of things," she says. "He doesn't need to be bothered with my troubles." We know what that means. We know that this whole stinking moment has become just a placeholder for her. And we know that having no loyalty and being disloyal are two completely different things.

Later, a story circulated that her husband first caught wind of the modeling when he was looking over one of his shipmate's shoulders at a magazine. And, without a doubt, there stood his wife. And he must have hoped it was only a hobby, one of those things that just happens, and not some new scheme of hers. Then, on a leave after Japan surrendered, he came home briefly before he was to ship out again, this time to Shanghai. He found his young bride was now a full-fledged model, using a new name, Marilyn Monroe, and talking of a possible film contract with Twentieth Century-Fox. His mother had tried to tell him. She hadn't been happy watching her daughter-in-law rush out of the house on weekends and at all hours to pose in swimsuits for magazines. Nor did she appreciate how her daughter-in-law abdicated all responsibility for her bills in favor of buying clothes and accessories that she claimed were necessary for her latest line of work. And there are lots of stories, and lots of accounts, but it seems most convincing that her newfound sense of purpose didn't match his. We can hear the argument now: "You're not the girl I married." "I am. I've just got something to focus on." "And your husband isn't enough? . . . Why are you being so bitchy?" "I'm sorry I'm not like your old beauty queen girlfriend." We can hear it because we've heard some form of it a million times over. But what we can't hear is what it means for her to be seen. And how she's always believed that nobody ever sees her quite right, and that maybe now that will change.

Not too long after she quit Radioplane, her photographs began showing up in magazines. Then she showed up in bit parts on the movie screen.

The funny thing is that one girl, Rita, always doubted that the *she* in the photos was the *she* who had worked here. We show Rita a picture in a magazine. Then point to the chair where she used to sit. "Right there," we say, nodding. "She's the one who sat right there."

Rita squints her eyes, trying to remember. Put it all into place. Finally she shakes her head no. "That's not the same girl," she says. "You're mixing it all up. You're goofing her up with someone else."

"No," we say, "no." We're laughing a little. Partly at Rita's insistence. And partly at a weird pride we've taken on. Most of us don't really approve of what she's done, especially considering the risk her husband faced in the South Pacific. We know opportunities come and go, and that there are proper moments in which to grab them, and perhaps what really threw us was how out of the blue it came, and how in retrospect it seems she was just lying in wait, always on call, for that one opportunity to change her life. So while her timing might be in question, we do quietly root for her. Why? Because despite all our higher grounds, she's there and we're still here.

Rita will not let up. She grabs the magazine out of our hands, flipping the pages quickly. (Now here's an odd thing: despite the cavernous setting of the hangar, in which sounds are always in competition, and where whispers nearly always rise into shouts, we can hear every page turn, as though a giant bird is beating its wings above our heads.) "Here," Rita says, "here." She shoves the magazine in our faces. We look at the picture. There she is, posing on the beach. Sitting in front of the receding tide, in a two-piece bathing suit, her right hand pinching the top, as if holding it up. She doesn't have that sad look anymore. She looks alive and almost carefree. The youth practically bursts out of her. It's as if being seen by the lens has cured her. But maybe the tragedy to all this, at least from our perspective, is how much she looks as though she believes the sadness will be gone forever.

"It's not even the right name," Rita says. "A totally different name. A totally different person."

"Okay," we say. "Okay." There's no strength left to pursue the argument. But to some degree Rita is right. She is a totally different person.

1951: Norwalk State Hospital, Norwalk, CA

The halls of Norwalk State Hospital: flat and dull, with floors that are mopped clean on the hour, and swept in between, looking like they've never been walked on, other than the black scuff marks that a loosely dragged mop head can't scrub out. There's always whispered talk among the staff. Whispers. (Always whispers.) The kind in which plans are made. After a while the whispering has the sound of conspiracy. In essence, all the patients are the same, because crazy is the same. It's just different shapes and sizes. There's a little fat man, mostly bald but crowned by an even ring of hair, and he likes to twirl in the middle of the floor, with his shirttails arranged so that his belly hangs out, shifting and tumbling, not sucked in for anyone anymore. And when the mood hits him right, and the watch is lax, his clothes start to come off piece by piece, and soon he's just a naked blob, spinning in circles, occasionally slapping down on his prick, which has hardened out of reflex, hitting it like it is a lever that will make him spin faster. Meanwhile, the talkers and the mumblers sit in the corners. They hold court with themselves, muttering invectives and regrets, the spite aimed at whomever looks at them, except for the pretty nurse's aides (although eventually they too will be implicated). The talkers and mumblers usually are old, committed so long ago they believe they have always been in Norwalk State Hospital. No memories of ever being children. (As if one could just appear in a state hospital.) They exist in a relative hush. Noise is the sound of disorder. Expressions are a sign of failure. But dig under that quiet, or at least get somewhere beneath it, and you'll hear something deafening. Like one of those whistles that only a dog hears, that drops it to its belly, unable to continue on.

Think about that.

Marilyn thinks about it every time she visits her mother.

Especially when she leaves. Falling down across the backseat of the town car. Hands cupped over her ears. Trying to silence the devastating pitch.

Maybe they ought to have their own wing at Norwalk State Hospital.

The Baker-Grainger Ward.

The Grainger-Baker Center.

It could be dedicated to the two women who raised her: her mother, Gladys Baker, and her grandmother, Delia Grainger.

Gladys must have known what this was like, walking through hospital corridors that smelled somewhere between stale and sterile, afraid to see her mother, because who would want to see her mother that way (especially when her mother was in fact that way). It was 1927 and all the world was talking about floods in Mississippi, and Sacco and Vanzetti being executed, and bombings in Bath Township, Michigan, and Charles Lindbergh. Gladys wanted to tell Delia about a new picture called *The Jazz Singer*, a talkie that was supposed to change every way people thought about the pictures. She wanted to tell her that. Because at least she had the movies with her mother. That one place where they could dissolve away together. But when she saw Delia sitting on the edge of her bed, grimacing and bending her fingers back one by one, Gladys was tempted to leave. Turn and walk away from her mother forever. She saw the rage (or at least the memory of the rage, which, in and of itself, was as real as the rage). It floated around her mother, seducing her. It was the same rage that had smashed glasses and plates against the floor. That verbally assaulted. That had kept anybody from ever coming over to the house. That hit Gladys's baby daughter, and, according to the little girl, also had tried to smother her with a pillow when a directive wasn't understood. That's what Gladys saw. She had to look away, terrified she'd also see the potential in herself. And while she hadn't ever physically lashed out at her daughter, Gladys had sometimes gazed at her and, for no reason, broken into a jag of tears.

Standing outside her mother's room at Norwalk, Gladys wanted so badly not to be related to Delia. Wanted it all to be a mistake. A clerical error. In the room, she sat down on the bed beside her mother. Out of instinct and habit, Gladys held her elbows akimbo, pointed outward as potential defenders. Delia grunted, then started coughing, bringing something up in her throat. When she was done she swallowed, yanked on her fingers, and tapped her foot twice on the floor.

Gladys stared into the hallway, unable to bring herself to look at her mother. And in a shaky voice that could not steady itself to normal, Gladys started talking about *The Jazz Singer*. Treated her mother as though she were listening. Going over all the minutiae, telling her about Al Jolson, May McAvoy, and making pretend plans for them to go downtown and see it together. When she was done, Gladys stood, saying it was time to go. She leaned forward as though about to kiss her mother's cheek, but stopped short, not wanting to get too close. Delia was like a fragile curio; the slightest touch might explode her into a thousand pieces.

Gladys walked the hallway, cataloging it the way she always did, trying to lodge the details of the hospital deep into her memory. One day her own mind would give in. It was part of her heritage. And when it did she'd want to know how Norwalk operated. So she sopped it up. Tried to store up as much as she could. Hoping that when she eventually needed it, the setup would make a little bit of sense.

Maybe a wing would not be enough.

Maybe the whole hospital. On a movie star's earnings it was possible. Maybe even an obligation. After all, it was a question of legacy. At least three generations deep.

It's supposed to be cheery in Norwalk. That's their word, *cheery*. It is a part of the overall therapeutic treatment, based on the belief that a positive environment makes for a positive mind. In the crowded hospital, the rules are all enumerated, as are the patients. How else could order possibly be kept? The nurses and hospital staff follow their training and, unless circumstances dictate otherwise, always speak in positive terms. Only the doctors avoid this routine. Crouched over their steel clipboards, listening for facts and scratching out orders, they have little time for such theatrics. They are the orchestrators. The composers. It's not their job to perform. In accordance with the emphasis on positivity, some patients are encouraged to take day trips with their families. Getting out and interacting with the world can create a feeling of normalcy. And so Marilyn takes her mother to lunch. They sit on a deck of a restaurant in Whittier. Gladys is hunched, hiding her face as though she's being watched. Having hardly spoken, she suddenly glances around and busts out: *You have to get me out of there*. She doesn't look at her daughter; it isn't clear she even knows who she is. Throughout lunch she only picks at the fried potatoes, saying, *You seem like a nice enough lady, and I know you won't take me back*. When they finish, and the car is driving back toward the hospital, her mother goes completely silent, only the occasional shifting, or a throat clearing and a grunt. Gladys squints and balls her fists as though she might explode, then stares out the window, watching the city go by, frame by frame, as if gawking at somebody else's memory. It's only when the car pulls into the long driveway that Gladys says, *I figured you weren't the type I could ever trust*. And as they walk toward the nurses' station, Marilyn keeps her head low, afraid that any eye contact might reduce her to tears. The nursing assistant comes over from behind the desk, a big black woman, and takes Gladys's hand, and with a large smile, she speaks with the enthusiasm of a waiting parent: "Oh, Mrs. Baker, don't you look lovely and refreshed. It is *so* good to have you home!"

March 8, 1952: Villa Nova Restaurant, Los Angeles

The cab arrives at the Villa Nova about fifteen minutes late, but Joe still feels prompt. He walks under the canopy and through the heavy wood door, shutting out the roar of Sunset Boulevard. As he strolls behind the maître d', he senses eyes being cast in his direction. It would be easier if they kept their stares to themselves. A little privacy is all he's hoped for since he retired last season. Making his way straight for the back table, he keeps his head low, his eyes focused on the floor. Someone says, "Hey Joe," but he doesn't look up, only purses his lips into a smile and keeps moving; he's been anticipating this night for weeks. He just hates that it has to be so public.

The dinner was arranged by a studio publicist named David March, who ran a photo shoot featuring Marilyn and another ballplayer, Philadelphia A's left fielder Gus Zernial. Joe had phoned March, saying that as long as he was brokering meetings between Marilyn and baseball players, then he wanted in, too. He knew March would comply—people like him always wanted Joe on their side. March expressed concern that

Marilyn might not accept, she was funny about doing things on her own terms, and not to take it personal. Try, Joe told him. It took a few back-and-forths. A little negotiating. But March finally sold it to Marilyn as a combination blind date/double date. It was best that way, he told Joe. She wasn't much interested in sports.

March and his date are seated all the way in the back, in one of the red leather booths. She twists her whole torso when she turns to greet Joe. He thinks it makes her look phony. Like she thinks she's some kind of sophisticate, so proper. Even her bright red lipstick bugs him. A little much for what is basically a high-priced spaghetti joint.

March stands, shakes Joe's hand, and offers a seat. Joe stares at the table, wondering where Marilyn is and where she will sit, but says nothing; instead he scoots into the left side of the booth, in front of March's half-filled water glass, staying near the end.

March says, "She's not here yet."

"I can see that," Joe says. "I can tell."

March keeps watch for Marilyn down the narrow restaurant corridor, peering toward the front door between waiters with plates of steaming pasta. She's nearly an hour and a half late. The candles on the tables have since been lit; the room has an evening glow. He's run out of excuses. All he can do is order a second round of martinis for the table. But Joe doesn't partake; martinis seem pretentious. Plus he prefers a clear head for when she comes. He wants to be at his best. He requests a refill of water, after which he takes a teaspoon and fishes out the ice cubes, drops them onto his red linen napkin, and then, folding it in half, watches the cloth darken.

Excusing himself, March declares he's going to check up front to see if she called. He bumps the table as he stands. Joe's water sloshes near the rim. "It's probably just . . ." March says. "You know how easily the business can throw off a schedule. Especially in a production."

Joe doesn't say a thing, keenly aware of how uncomfortable his silence makes his companions.

"Just give me a few moments," March says. And he walks through the core of the Villa Nova, visible only by the flickering candles.

A few minutes after being left alone with Joe, the date turns to him, as if the quiet kills her. "You don't still play ball, do you?"

He shakes his head.

"I didn't think so, but I thought it was recent. It was recent, right? David says you have a TV show, on CBS. A baseball show?"

"NBC."

"Oh," she says, "NBC."

He squeezes the napkin, making what's left of the ice completely melt.

She says she has a friend who worked at NBC, and she wonders if Joe knows her, although she can't remember the exact division, and he tries to keep from yawning while she rattles off names of industry people that don't mean a thing. Finally, she stops. After peering around the restaurant, she leans in, gripping the stem of her glass. "It's a little rude, don't you think," she says, "to keep people waiting so long. Between you and me, I don't know how long I'm good for."

Joe doesn't reply. He's willing to wait it out all night.

Once she enters, there is no question how her presence changes the room. Like a giant exhalation. Dressed in black, she commands the attention of the Villa Nova, strolling with slow purpose until she reaches the table. It's as though the whole restaurant has brightened, the candles' flames standing taller. There is something light about her, at once ghostly and cartoonish. Without saying anything, she puts her palms flat on the table-top and leans forward, as though exhausted, looking for a drink. He's struck by how young she looks, almost like a little girl playing dress-up. And he watches as she slowly takes off her coat and pauses, letting the restaurant see how tightly the fabric of her dress clenches her chest, instinctively annoyed at her showboating but forgiving it as a vulnerability. "Sorry for being late," she says, but offers no excuses other than needing a little extra time for her yoga. "And you didn't even order me a drink yet? Shame on you, David." She edges herself around the table, just about falling back into her seat on the bench, as March calls the waiter over. "I guess this is my spot," she says, smiling at Joe; then she makes a comment about the placement of the center polka dot on his tie, in a tone that comes out somewhere between bravado and awkwardness.

March formally introduces them, reiterating, *Joe DiMaggio. From the New York Yankees.* She cocks her head, trying to recall why she knows his name. "Of course," she says, "of course." She confesses she really doesn't know much about baseball, as though saying that absolves her from having to have any conversation with him. And for a moment the table has a perfect silence.

The waiter arrives with a bottle of champagne and four glasses. "Thank goodness," she says, breaking the quiet. She turns to March and begins talking shop about the film she's negotiating. And as she prattles on about the movie business, Joe senses himself falling behind. As useless as March's date. So he tries to regain his focus. Breathe. Put all the distractions and chatter out of his mind.

He can tell she really has nothing to say to these people. It's all just surface noise. But the difference is that she's been better trained on how to make them feel as though they're interesting. And most maddening and insulting to him is they obviously don't give a shit about what she says, only that she's saying it to *them*. So they keep her talking. And it makes him sick, watching that. For a moment he wishes he could just lean across the table and tell David March and his date to shut the crap up, and let Marilyn enjoy her meal, and just be. Can't they see she's just a child, and not some blow-up toy? Not everything has to be about desperate business interactions. But then he would lose his mental edge. And he knows the difference between winning and losing is all in your head.

She turns to Joe and says she's sorry. "This must be a bore. It's just that I don't know much about sports." He says it's okay, and dips his spoon into his water, stirring and looking for ice shards.

Out of nowhere, Mickey Rooney approaches the table. March and his date look right to Marilyn, expecting he's come to say hello to her. But Rooney zeroes in on Joe, rubbing his hands together, lacing his fingers in and out of each other. He says he was just seated a few tables over, and he couldn't believe what he saw when he looked across the room. The Yankee Clipper, on the Sunset Strip of all places. And Rooney starts in about the Yankees, and he wants to know what Joe thinks their chances are. Will Ford and Lopat win twenty this year? Is Mantle the real deal? Each time Joe pauses after giving a polite answer, Rooney looks around the table and declares Joe to be the greatest athlete of all time. He tells the table he still can't believe the "streak," that baseball itself might have hit its peak when Joe broke that record.

From the corner of his eye, Joe can see Marilyn watching with a new interest. Just like March and his date, Marilyn has the keen ability to home in on the spot where the attention is, and to move herself toward its center. It's the gift of the Hollywood players. She scoots in a bit closer to Joe, putting her palm on the bench for support as she moves over, just beside his leg. He moves toward her a little, just enough to feel the heat coming off her hand.

After Rooney leaves, Marilyn turns all her attention to Joe. He understands she now sees him as being something more than just a ballplayer. *Tell me how to hit a baseball. What's it like to hit a home run? Have you ever won the championship of baseball? Do you know Babe Ruth?* She can't control the phoniness. It's that conditioned. But it doesn't bother him. He knows what the entertainment business can do to a person. Looking at her, he doesn't see a movie star or even the sexy pose from her publicity photos. He sees just an ordinary girl who's been hamstrung and seduced into acting like some kind of hand puppet, and who is all the more miserable for it. Someone who needs to be looked out for.

And as she prattles on at him, he stares past her into the darkening room, his eyes glazing. In his head, he's imagining taking her up to San Francisco, where he could free her from the cycle of mutual sycophancy by giving her a quiet, respectable life. Show her a routine. Home meals. Quiet nights. Allow her the freedom to be just a homemaker. He'd offer her the chance to let her true nature come out—a decent, caring girl. Because he knows what it's like to be barely out of childhood, and still owned by the grownup world. The recognition is almost heartbreaking. But the need to protect is even more compelling.

She keeps talking at him about Hollywood nonsense. He barely says another word through dinner, instead slowly turning his thoughts into plans.

Finally, she stops for a moment and says, "You don't have much to say on these topics, do you?" which, at least to Joe, couldn't make him feel more connected to her. And that much more committed.

January 14, 1954: City Hall, San Francisco

On the day of her wedding to Joe DiMaggio at San Francisco City Hall, Marilyn's horoscope in the *San Francisco Chronicle* reads: "Ferreting out best way to improve emotional delights and getting more desirable system in practical relations with others yields big returns, by quickly putting conclusion into execution."

Page one of the same paper warns of shifting weather. The weather bureau forecasts a cold winter storm coming down from Alaska, predicting occasional rains and cooler temperatures—somewhere between 51 and 56 degrees.

The wedding was supposed to be a secret, but it's not much of one. Having been suspended by Twentieth Century-Fox the past week for failing to show up for filming on a new picture called *The Girl in Pink Tights*,

Marilyn has been staying in the Marina district with Joe's sister. It was the role that bothered her, a lead she referred to as a "cliché-spouting bore in pink tights [who] was the cheapest character I ever read in a script." There were rumbles of agreement within the studio, but the front office had no intention of letting Marilyn Monroe dictate the terms of how the studio's decisions and its movies were made. She took the suspension with some pride, and went north. With Joe's encouragement, she is willing to be out of the business altogether, if that's how they see her. Rumors of a wedding have already circulated. The speculation is that one took place somewhere in Nevada. Another bit of scuttlebutt places it in Hollywood. And among many watchers, suggestions of a settled domestic life in San Francisco have made the rounds. It's rumored that Joe has had it with show business, telling television producer Jack Barry that he won't do another TV gig like *The Joe DiMaggio Show* again, and, following the nonsense of *The Girl in Pink Tights*, he's encouraged Marilyn to do the same with Fox. Neither of them needs it anymore. The word is they are cashing in Hollywood for an ordinary life.

Gossip reporters claim the couple now spends their evenings at home in front of the television. The occasional night out finds them in the back of Joe's restaurant. Eating quietly. Hardly conversing.

The press arrives at Municipal Judge Charles S. Peery's chambers well ahead of the 1:00 PM scheduled ceremony, as do somewhere in the neighborhood of five hundred people, turning an otherwise respectful city hall office and entryway into what local columnist Art Hoppe deems a "madhouse."

Then in comes the couple through the Polk Street doors, slowly moving across the marble floors. Their presence alone seems to light the gilded trim and molding of the great hall. The groom wears a dark blue suit with a checked tie. The bride teeters between city style and homemaker elegance in a brown broadcloth suit with an ermine collar; her nails are freshly done with a natural polish, and her fake eyelashes, long and dark, obscure the disquiet in her eyes.

All of city hall has stopped. The secretaries, the bureaucrats, the local legislators. Paperwork stays on their desks. Telephones ring, unanswered. No one can say why; there is just the sense of splendor in the building. Someone will lean across a service counter in the real estate department on the third floor and say to his colleague that it feels as if the earth is stuck, paused on its axis, and then they'll both, along with the others in the division, spill into the hallway in front of the judge's chambers.

The only person who can't stop working is a deputy county clerk named David Dunn. He's running from office to office with a blank marriage license, unable to find access to a free typewriter so Judge Peery can have the paperwork in hand once the nuptials begin.

The couple walks two steps ahead of their guests, a tightly knit train of an entourage: Mr. and Mrs. Tom DiMaggio (Joe's brother), Mr. and Mrs. Francis "Lefty" O'Doul (Joe's first baseball manager from the Seals), and Mr. and Mrs. Reno Barsocchini (Joe's restaurant partner).

The *Examiner* doesn't neglect to report that Marilyn was raised in an orphanage.

"Are you excited, Marilyn?"

"Oh, you *know* it's more than that."

"How many children are you going to have, Joe?"

"We'll have at least one. I'll guarantee that."

The day of the marriage, the *San Francisco Chronicle* runs its column called "Hints for Homemakers." It offers many fine bits of advice, including

* Always rinse your eggbeater under cold water right after you use it.
* Next time you have a cod-liver oil stain to remove, try this: Sponge the stain with glycerin, then launder as usual.
* Every kitchen should be supplied with a dozen dish and glass towels, six dishcloths, and at least four pot holders. Have two of the pot holders large and heavy. The other two may be smaller and lighter in weight.
* Before putting your vacuum cleaner away, wind

the cord loosely. Tension may cause fine wires inside the cord to break.

It's impossible to see behind her heavily made-up eyes that she is only twenty-seven. In a roomful of reporters, seated across from her husband-to-be, nearly a dozen years his junior, she's like a little girl at her mother's dressing table for the first time, smudging on makeup, almost clownlike in bright reds and silvery blues. On the day of her wedding in city hall, she's but one of a million babes who suddenly finds herself living in the middle of her wishes, unable to stop wondering whether it's equally possible to will them away.

"Marilyn. Miss Monroe. Are you planning on giving up acting for homemaking? Care to comment?"

"What difference does it make, I'm suspended . . ."

"This is no time to talk of suspensions. We've got to get going. We got to put a lot of miles behind us."

"Is that right, Joe? Tell us, tell your fans, where you two going, Joe? Where's the honeymoon gonna be?"

"North. South. West. And east."

Sometime after 1:30 PM, Judge Peery's chambers are cleared. The couple enters, and waits. Reporters are moved to an office just outside the room, and the swelling crowd jams the hallway.

One reporter, standing tiptoe on a desk, is able to glimpse into the chambers through the transom. An anxious silence quells the area, as the report of his observation is anticipated. "They're not getting married," he calls to the crowd. "They're drinking martinis." A cheer goes up, if only because it seems as though a cheer is in order.

Deputy county clerk David Dunn is still running from office to office, blank license in hand, trying to find a machine to type on.

That same day, at about the same time the wedding is taking place, Albert Einstein's grandson is pleading guilty to petty-theft charges in Pittsburgh, California. According to the *San Francisco Examiner*, the twenty-three-year-old, along with an accomplice, was arrested "in the act of pilfering money from a soft drink dispenser coin box." The amount was $1.10. They were set free on bail, to await their sentencing from the district judge. The judge's final sentence is not reported in the paper. And there appear to be no reporters on site to get the reaction of the defendant or his family. Receiving attention is all a matter of perspective.

Deputy county clerk David Dunn runs into the judge's chambers, reportedly having to "beat his way through the crowd." He comes back out within a minute or two. The blank license is still in his hand. A "great howl" begins to swell, with the crowd chanting, "Machine. Machine. Machine."

Once Dunn finally locates a typewriter at an empty desk, he types out the license in duplicate, carefully and hurriedly, looking at each letter as it strikes the page; not in admiration, more in a submissive fear.

The ceremony starts at 1:45 PM. It ends at 1:48 PM.

An advertisement in the daily paper offering new mixes from Duncan Hines claims that Hines himself has "achieved what he set out to do: bring you homemade quality without the work of making homemade cake."

Following the ceremony, the couple poses for photos and answers some questions. They kiss playfully, shy away, until a news photographer suggests one more for the paper. "Aw, shucks," Joe says. He looks down, then at her, and shrugs, "Well, okay, then." The photos have a certain intimacy to them, as though capturing the center of a raw moment between very public people. It is that privacy exposed that unsettles. The way she smiles unsurely. As if she understands the expectations of happiness but can't quite call them up. And Joe, looking oddly flat-footed, more proud than joyful, at times kisses her the way passionless parents would kiss at the marriage of their daughter, utterly practiced. But there is one picture in which both his hands grip her back while her left hand nearly rests on his lapel as though it might pull away at a moment's notice, and neither looks as though they're really holding on, and she seems to be slightly leaned back, stretching her face out to meet his, which is cocked and pushed forward; and what's there is not romance but the belief in it, the willingness to try. After the sounds of the shutters fire and die, Joe pulls away. "Let's go," he says. "Let's go."

"I met him two years ago on a blind date in Los Angeles, and a couple of days ago we started talking about this."

As she spoke about *this* to eager reporters, the *Examiner* reported, "DiMaggio puffed nervously on a cigarette."

It was more accident than miscalculation that found them in the real estate department on the third floor. They'd been trying to leave the building, figuring they could move down the two flights of stairs and into the waiting blue Cadillac that would whisk them up McAllister Street toward the Marina. They were taken somewhat by surprise at the relentlessness of the press and the fans who began tailing them down the hallway. The pace hastened, and soon they were engaged in a full game of chase. From above it must have looked like a wedged school of fish moving through the halls, with the newlyweds at the point, turning corners and circling around, knowing they had to give up on the stairs when it became clear they too would be jammed. They dashed around the circumference of the third floor, her heels sometimes catching on the marble, opening doors and closing them, pulling up short just before getting trapped into corners, doubling back, hoping to find the elevator that would drop them straight to the first floor, forced to navigate less by instinct and knowledge and more by adrenaline.

Cornered in the real estate department office, unsure of what to do (Marilyn without her coat, accidentally left behind in the judge's chambers), they stared through the small rectangular window in the door, wires crisscrossed into diamond shapes. In the glass, the couple could see their reflections, a sort of waxy version of themselves laid over the swelling crowd outside. The room felt deadened, as though it were a bubble of silence. Already it was understood not only that this protective bubble was temporary but also that it was bound to pop, because that's what bubbles do—they pop.

They took smalls steps backward until they were stopped against the service counter, neatly arranged with organized stacks of forms at each end and a clipboard with a sign-in sheet in the middle. Pods of empty desks were abandoned behind them. On one desk a phone rang but stopped after a single ring, the bell momentarily hanging and then fading like a chime.

She pushed her back harder against the counter. A black plastic nameplate fell to the floor.

They waited like hostages. Hands pressed against the smooth blond wood. No words. Just slow breaths. A whistling through his nose. They looked once at each other and, as though on cue, nodded. On an unspoken count of three they rushed at the door, pulling it open and running straight into the mob, hands held and eyes closed, like warriors making their last stand against a force dozens of times their size, not even bothering to dodge and weave a path through the wave of bullets, believing only in the hope that there's always a way out.

One more piece of advice from the *San Francisco Chronicle*'s "Hints for Homemakers":

* A quick rub of Vaseline keeps corks from sticking in bottles of liquid cement, polishes, and glue. And a dab of glue on the knot will seal the ends of cord when there isn't enough to knot securely.

September 1954: Los Angeles

Marilyn Monroe was intended to be about the wanting, never the having. And now Joe, representing all the men in the world who've wanted you, suddenly is in your home with his hands on your body and his breath on your neck. To be fair, you initially did find the storybook marriage intoxicating, in part due to the improbability of that being your life, the little orphan girl of the crazy mom now envied for doing something so big as to marry a superstar ballplayer. But too soon he wants to change things. Remove you from the spotlight. Chastise you for always having to act like Marilyn Monroe. The boundaries get confused. And he tells you that you need to stay home and be a wife, and in fairness you can see that he really does value that role by the way he points to his sisters and his mother as prime examples of womanhood, but this storybook is starting to make less and less sense because he really doesn't want you to be the main character in it anymore, and you can feel the rage inside him when he visits the set of *The Seven Year Itch* on Lexington and Fifty-Second in New York and sees you showing your legs take after take and flirting with the gathering crowd and the press in between, and he walks off the set, heading straight back to the St. Regis Hotel, where, even though he barely says a word when you return, you can see the outrage building, almost expanding in his gut, until he bursts out that he doesn't understand why you do this, and why you don't want to be freed from this degrading career and realize the opportunity he's giving you to have a settled life as a homemaker.

And now sometimes he won't talk to you for days, sometimes a week at a time, and you ask him what's wrong and he tells you to leave him alone, and it's hard to know what's what, only that he bristles every time you talk about a potential new movie deal or magazine shoot, and he seems to puff larger, as though it's a further betrayal; and on occasion he reminds you how much you need him, how he protects you, and you'll say you don't want his protection, and that's when he shuts down—all he ever knows how to do is get disturbed and indignant when you're lousy with grief; and you run into the bedroom and slam the door and lie on the bed, waiting to hear his footsteps leaving the house, remembering being taken to the Los Angeles Orphans Home Society, crying as you were led through the door, trying to explain to whomever would listen, *Please, please don't make me go inside. I'm not an orphan, my mother's not dead. I'm not an orphan—it's just that she's sick in the hospital and can't take care of me.*

November 5, 1954: West Hollywood, Los Angeles

The suit was settled four years after the incident, and a little less than a year after the actual filing. Florence Kotz, a forty-year-old secretary from Los Angeles, named several defendants—most notably Joe DiMaggio and Frank Sinatra. According to a wire report, her suit claimed that she was "seized with hysteria when the defendants allegedly broke down her apartment door and flashed lights into her eyes on the night of November 5, 1954." Kotz asked the Los Angeles Superior Court for $200,000 in damages. She settled for $7,500.

It took three years for Virginia Blasgen, owner of the apartment building where Kotz lived at 754 North Kilkea Drive, to be awarded a default judgment of $100 from the small claims court in Los Angeles for the damage done to the apartment door. In addition, she received $5.75 for court costs.

But that night of November 5, years before any legal settlements, Virginia Blasgen has been looking out her window on and off for the past hour. She initially sees only two men hanging around the front of her rental property across the street, at 754 North Kilkea. Her father built that apartment house, and now she owns it. Eventually it will go to her boy. She has to keep an eye out. It isn't just property she's protecting. It's a future.

She parts the curtain further with her right hand; her view is partially blocked by a large elm. The taller man stamps around, looking agitated, slightly unguarded. They seem determined and confident. Almost hammy. The "little one," she'll later recall, "was jumping up and down, and looking at me and smiling."

The rental is a triplex, with a small studio on the bottom and two larger apartments on top. It's Mission style, typical of the quiet residential neighborhood, with a brilliant green lawn, not so easy to maintain under the shade of the giant elm. One of the upstairs units is rented out to an actress named Sheila Stewart. She seemed like a nice girl when Virginia showed her the efficiency, responsible and clean. She reported having steady work, and came armed with the first and last months' rent, ready to take the place. Virginia mentioned some concern about her being an actress, inferring a different lifestyle standard, and Sheila Stewart assured her she was of a serious nature—that when she wasn't auditioning she prized her classes and her rest. Sheila Stewart has so far lived up to that claim. But seeing the men gather in front of the building makes Virginia wonder if Sheila Stewart hasn't taken on another prize.

DiMaggio says he's not fooling around any longer. He wants to bust right through the door. It's dark and it's nearing midnight, and the sky is clear, almost invisible. Under the umbrella glow of a street lamp, he leans against his Cadillac convertible, his shoulders pressed against the canvas top, talking at Barney Ruditsky, a private investigator, and Phil Irwin, a retired cop who works for Ruditsky. They've both arrived within the last fifteen minutes, along with Henry Sanicola and DiMaggio's friend Bill Karen, who wait quietly in the backseat of the car. Warming himself up, Sinatra lounges in the front passenger's seat, jangling the car keys and tapping his foot.

DiMaggio's insisting that if indeed she's inside there, they might as well go in now. His muscles tense. His entire body constricts. "I don't know why we just don't go in and bust this guy up," he says. Shadows from the lamplight burrow into the lines in his face, aging him. "Make sure he's the one that gets fucked, and not her."

Ruditsky speaks in a low voice, trying to draw DiMaggio closer. Quiet him down. Bring on some calm. He's trailed enough women to be able to predict a man's reaction—especially that of one so recently and publicly humiliated. "Better to think out what we should do," he suggests. "What we're after."

"I know what we should do. What I'm after."

Sinatra leans out the window, elbow on the door. "I tell you what you should be doing, Philly," he tells

Irwin. "You should be helping the old detective calm Joe down into a logical plan."

DiMaggio snaps back at Sinatra that his plan is to see the fear in this guy's face. "I want to hear his skull cracking on top of her. Like an egg."

"Well, I'm sure you three will work it out," Sinatra says. He slides over into the driver's seat. "I'm going to move this car over a couple of blocks. Out of sight. No need to make it too easy on the cops."

Sinatra and DiMaggio were eating at Villa Capri when the call came in from Ruditsky. Irwin had spotted her. She'd gone into the house on North Kilkea they had under surveillance, the one they were sure was the cover for her affair. Sinatra took the call from the maître d'. He didn't have a good feeling about where this was heading. They had knocked back a few over dinner, and though not fully anticipating this development, it was as if they'd been preparing for it. DiMaggio had been jawing on and on about her. Knowing she was putting the hump on that clown, Hal Schaefer. A stinking vocal coach. And a fucking queer, if he didn't know better. And he was just supposed to sit here accepting it because a court had granted her an *interlocutory decree*; but that meant there was still a waiting period before the divorce was legal, therefore she was still his wife, and if she was still his wife, then she didn't get to do that kind of shit . . . And he went at Sinatra nonstop until the phone call, never betraying an emotion, just getting more stiff and more wooden with every thought.

But that was dinner.

After confirming that Ruditsky was certain, Sinatra said he'd take it to DiMaggio.

Just to be clear: The interlocutory divorce decree was granted to Marilyn Monroe by the Los Angeles Superior Court on grounds of mental cruelty.

Sinatra comes walking around the corner, dancing a mock jitterbug as he approaches the boys, Sanicola and Karen in tow. Irwin stands alone, a cigarette between his fingers, pointing the red ember toward the shadow where Ruditsky and DiMaggio huddle.

Ruditsky looks as though he's working hard to keep his cool. He's no piece-of-shit private eye. Making his reputation as a New York City cop in '28, he went undercover beneath a bedsheet on a slab in a Second Street Turkish bathhouse, with his piece on his stomach, just waiting to bust up the so-called "Poison Ivy" gang. After that he collared the likes of Legs Diamond and Dutch Schultz, and the main West Side thugs, such as the "Pear Button" gang. He came west after the TV studios decided to make a series, *The Lawless Years*, based on a memoir he'd published. He worked as a technical consultant on the show and then moved on to movies, making sure the police and criminals were portrayed with some degree of accuracy. The PI work came on the side, only the right cases when the right people asked. He doesn't quite know why he has to answer to DiMaggio. After all, it was Sinatra who hired him. Yankee Clipper or no Yankee Clipper, Ruditsky has little patience for this kind of amateur bullshit about cracking skulls. "But I'm telling you," DiMaggio is saying, "I'm not fooling around here any longer. Let's just kick the door in."

Ruditsky says, "We have to make it count for something."

"No need to worry on that."

"Pictures, for example . . . Something to hold over her, rather than giving her something to hold over you. A good photo will be worth thousands to you, Joe. Your lawyer shows it to her lawyer, and there you go. Thousands saved." Ruditsky motions for Irwin to get the camera out of the trunk, mouthing to remember to charge the flash.

"I don't like this," DiMaggio says. "Don't like this at all . . . Frank, do you like this?"

"I think we should listen to Barney."

DiMaggio looks at Ruditsky. "He says I should listen to you."

"We get the pictures, and then we go. You'll have everything you need."

"But I want them to be afraid."

"Afraid?"

"When I kick down that door, I want to see it in their eyes."

"Frank," Ruditsky says. "He says he still wants to kick down the door."

"So let him kick the door down."

Ruditsky pauses. He draws in a breath. He speaks, seemingly without exhaling. "Okay, we kick down the door. But just for effect . . . It's just for effect . . . Then it stops when I go for the pictures."

"After we bust down the fucking door."

It's at about this point that Florence Kotz's complaint against the defendants begins.

The front door is heavy; dark, solid wood. It'll take a tank to smash it down. Ruditsky doesn't want to go through the front. He tells DiMaggio that's a bullshit plan. They'll be glowing under the street lamps and porch lights, might as well smile for the mug shots. Already he's noticed some neighbors peeking out their windows.

He orders the group to the side of the house. DiMaggio goes reluctantly. From there, they snake into the backyard, each holding the gate for the next, until Sinatra, the last of the bunch, passes through. "All clear," Sinatra announces, looking backward when he hears a cricket chirp.

Irwin whispers that the entrance doesn't look right. Maybe they ought to pause. Just to make sure. It feels funny going in this way.

"How about you not worry about plans," Ruditsky says. "And how about I stay the boss."

Sinatra smiles. "All clear," he says again.

Irwin carries the camera. Sanicola and Karen carry police flashlights, gripped as though they're shaking hands. DiMaggio holds a bat, a fact not lost on anyone.

Virginia Blasgen thinks the two well-dressed men look familiar, but out of place in the neighborhood. She pulls the drapes open a little wider. Steals a quick glance when they walk toward the elm. She puts a finger beneath her nose to hold back a sneeze and almost suffocates swallowing it. It comes to her. The short one, she'd swear, is Frank Sinatra, and the tall one is the ballplayer, Joe DiMaggio, Marilyn Monroe's husband.

Maybe Sheila Stewart's dedication has paid off.

Hold your breath, Ruditsky motions. Keep your voices down. And don't rattle the change in your pockets. Nobody needs the upstairs neighbors taking notice.

It's easy to picture Florence Kotz in her Murphy bed. With the closet door wide open and the frame pulled down, the mattress would take up the better part of the room. One can imagine a single end table pushed against the wall, holding an alarm clock with fluorescent hands, a small flexible reading light, and a glass half full of water. Covering her would be a brown cotton blanket that's snugly tucked beneath a rose-hemmed chenille bedspread; it *is* November. Sleeping soundly, long acclimated to the footsteps above her, maybe Florence stirs a little with the rattling outside the back door, shifting and rolling over to face the other way. Her Murphy bed has a solid frame; the mesh supports are still tight. It doesn't sag or squeak. She'd hardly notice her own movements. Nor would she notice the usual night sounds: screens banging with the breeze, car doors slamming, or the alley cats rummaging through the garbage cans.

But with the crash she's instantly awake. There is no processing. No evaluation. She's sitting upright in her bed, frozen in place as though chilled mercury streams through her veins. And she can hear feet stamping through her kitchen, crunching over the broken glass. There are voices. Hushed to a whisper, but not as though they're trying to conceal themselves; it's more that they're startled by the magnitude of their own presence in such small quarters. She's paralyzed. Darkness gives the only sense of safety. She considers if there is some way to push the Murphy bed back into the wall, folding herself inside. Maybe the intruders will go away as quickly as they came in. A single glance should tell them there is nothing of value in this apartment. But the predominant thought, and she's vaguely aware it's the least rational, is that she wishes they would stop walking over the broken glass. It will be impossible to get it all up. She won't be able to walk barefoot for months.

Two flashlights beam on her. Already she knows she won't remember what she saw. Only that the sound of her scream started to form in front of her. A protective wall that grew gigantic, pushing the intruders back and back and back, until there was nothing to see.

The apartment becomes still again, save for the familiar and expected noises. The footsteps above. The alley cats upsetting the trash can lids.

With the crash comes a shriek for help. Virginia Blasgen immediately dials the police and then instinctively rushes outside. It's dark. Damp. She just reacts, not even putting on her slippers. If she thought about it she would realize how cold her feet are against the dewed grass.

She assumes the shriek has come from Sheila Stewart's apartment. In this town, everyone understands that the starlet part of show business requires a good scandal, and Sheila probably has found herself in the middle of something that's too big for her. After this is settled, Virginia might have to ask her to leave. Her property is not the right stage for this kind of drama. She thinks this until another series of cries comes from Miss Kotz's bottom unit. And as Virginia starts to cross the street toward her rental unit, she hears men's voices.

She dashes back. Scampering across her lawn. Taking cover along the side of her house, under the shadows. The stucco is rough and raw against her back. Her feet numb. She tries not to breathe. Or make any sudden movements.

She hears the gate across the street rattle and slam. The men's whispers turn louder, and hurried.

With great care, she inches herself along the wall toward the corner of the house, bare heels aching from loose pebbles. From the corner she sees silhouettes. Long and cartoonish. Joe DiMaggio? Frank Sinatra? It's hard to make out anyone else. She closes her eyes, reciting all her options to herself, of which there seem to be few, if any. She's outnumbered, and hopelessly unprepared for this kind of situation. Stranded on the side of her building. Unable to get to Miss Kotz. Unable even to get back into her house. Where are the police? Her legs tremble, and though it isn't that cold, her teeth chatter. She squeezes her eyes tighter. Wishing all of them gone. That's the best option. Disappear off the block.

When Virginia opens her eyes, they are gone. Car doors slam several blocks away. She arches forward, peering across North Kilkea. Indeed, it's all over. As though they were never there.

All is normal again on this quiet West Hollywood street. Other than another piercing cry from Miss Kotz's apartment. And the distant sirens growing louder and louder.

Sinatra later denied he had anything to do with the matter. Said he'd come along for the ride, but then held back once he figured it was best to hold back. He never went through that gate on North Kilkea Drive. Never saw that woman screaming, upright in her bed. There are some lines you don't cross.

Virginia Blasgen's and Florence Kotz's memories contradict Sinatra's. But in the end the women's recollections amounted only to a reduced settlement and a new back door, presumably a little sturdier than the original.

While noted contextually in news accounts, rarely was it discussed that Marilyn, in fact, was upstairs in Sheila Stewart's apartment, drinking a cup of tea. One can imagine her there, taking refuge from the storm that has surged around her breakup with DiMaggio. Liberating and frightening all at once. But in this one little pause, over a steaming cup of mint tea, laughing with her friend, she can feel totally at ease, completely free to reinvent, without DiMaggio's hands sculpting her into postures she could never keep. It feels good. And she wants to savor the moment. She understands that the dread of aloneness will fill her in a matter of days.

In the early part of the evening, Sheila carries the teacups into the living room, pinching the saucers, walking deliberately so as not to spill. Just the smell of the mint tea is relaxing. Sheila hands Marilyn one cup, puts hers on the coffee table, and then falls into the couch.

Marilyn blows across the surface, pushing steam away. "You're lucky, Sheila," she says.

"Lucky?"

"Well, maybe fortunate. Maybe that's more what I mean."

Shelia laughs. "I'm not sure what you mean—fortunate or lucky."

Marilyn stops herself. She doesn't try to explain. Because she knows that what she means is that Sheila is lucky (or fortunate) not to be her. How lucky to be a serious and struggling actor, living quietly in a modest West Hollywood apartment. To have her determination guided by a sense of self. Then she realizes how preposterous that might sound, a combination of pejorative arrogance and obliviousness. She turns a little red. "Oh, nothing," Marilyn stumbles. "I don't even know what I mean half the time."

"Yes, I know what you mean. That is to say, *I* don't know what *I* mean half the time."

Leaning forward to sip her tea, Marilyn starts laughing. The tea spills onto the saucer. She balances the dish just enough to keep the hot water from dripping on her thigh.

Sheila looks at her. "See, you're lucky too."

And then they hear the crash downstairs, where a man who had once cherished her as a vulnerable innocent but has now cast her as a selfish whore is ready to show her and the world that what he knows can't be wrong.

July 27, 1962

Cal Neva Lodge, Crystal Bay, NV

Straddling the line that separates California from Nevada can bring different reactions. For some visitors to the Cal Neva Lodge it's amusement. A game of hopping back and forth, calling out silver, gold, silver, gold. For others there is a sense of symbolism, a slight elitism to being over the California line—that side where Sinatra keeps his cabin, along with five others, to form his own private compound. Sinatra calls Tahoe the "jewel of the Sierras," and it sounds so corny when he says it, but each time she visits and is reacquainted with the lake from her regular cabin, number three, she can't think of any word other than jewel, because that is what it's like (as corny as it sounds)—a big blue sapphire set in the most perfect ring of Sierra Mountains.

12:36 PM

Near the end of the afternoon flight up to Reno from Los Angeles, Pat Lawford leans forward in her lounge chair to talk with Marilyn. Her mollifying smile is reminiscent of a ward nurse's, not the typical staid expression one expects from President Kennedy's sister. They're in Frank Sinatra's plane, a business jet he's christened *El Dago* and furnished like a living room, complete with the couch Marilyn is sitting on, a piano, and one of Frank's own paintings of a big-eyed kid framed in gold and hanging on the paneled wall nearest the cockpit, a long vertical piece. It's an easy flight up north, no more than an hour and a half, to be capped by an hour drive to Sinatra's casino, the Cal Neva Lodge in Crystal Bay, built smack-dab on the state line that divides California and Nevada.

Pat whispers just loudly enough to be heard over the plane's chopping engine but quietly enough not to disturb her sleeping husband, Peter Lawford, slumped in the chair next to her. She asks if Marilyn's all right, noting that she looks a little pale. "Or maybe," Pat says, clarifying her thought, "you look a little in between."

Marilyn says she was napping earlier. She shrugs. "Sometimes, you know, the dreams take a little while to dissolve. That's probably all. Waking up. It *can* leave you a little in between."

Pat says, "I wanted to catch you early. Before it becomes public."

"Public?"

"Listen to me, Marilyn." Pat's voice drops further. "It's something I overheard right before we boarded. Something that concerns me."

Whether it's the rumble of the plane or the travel fatigue, Marilyn is having trouble catching everything Pat says. She edges toward Pat. Just when she's close enough to hear, the pilot announces they're preparing to land.

Peter wakes, shaking his head and rubbing the heels of his palms against his eyes. He groggily instructs both women to sit back. They sit back. Pat catches Marilyn's eye, glances at Peter, and then shakes her head. "It will have to wait until we're down and alone," Pat says. "Until then. When we can talk." And for that Marilyn's relieved. Why would she want more concerns? Isn't being free from them the main reason she's going away for the weekend?

She looks over Pat's shoulder at the cityscape of Reno abutting the treelined Sierra Nevadas. After the whole drama of working there on *The Misfits*, she'd like to reach down, pinch Virginia Street, and flick the whole city away.

Trying to push her voice across the aisle, Marilyn says to Pat, "You know, I really don't care for these landings. How it all closes in just so. Like going down a rabbit hole."

The plane quickly dips.

The landing gear creaks, and a slight stink of jet fuel washes through the cabin. When the plane turns and dips, it's all sky out the window.

"Pat," Marilyn says, loud enough to be heard. "Pat?"

"Yes, Marilyn."

"I won't forget."

"Forget?"

"That there's something you need to tell me. Your concern. I won't forget that. You'll tell me inside, Pat? When we reach the lodge?"

"When we reach the lodge."

"I won't forget. I promise you I won't forget." Although as she says this it occurs to her that she hopes she does.

The plane drops farther, and then goes into a brief holding pattern.

2:00 PM

He watches from the hill, hands on his hips, as though waiting in the on-deck circle. He's always been vigilant. Patient. As she scoots out of the station wagon after the Lawfords, gathering up her purse and valise, she glances behind her, across Highway 28, and sees Joe there, on a crest among the pines, halfway up, on the Nevada side. Her outfit matches the clarity of the Tahoe light—a green silk Pucci blouse, with long sleeves and a boat neck, and matching forest green slacks and shoes. Tired eyes are hidden behind the dark lenses of her cat-eye glasses.

The hillside is dried and brown, rocks and gravel and shrubbery exposed under the late summer sun. It's impossible to know how long he's been waiting, and exactly what he intends to do. Maybe he's just there to let her know he's watching. Or maybe to act as some totemic protector. Standing beside the car, she looks again. It's been almost eight years since the divorce. Even during her marriage to Arthur, Joe acted as though their being apart was nothing but a trial separation. He was confident she'd come around again. Give up all the New York monkey business and come back to who he knew she really was. With vigilance, he's hated anybody who puts crazy ideas in her head. He's blamed Hollywood, he's blamed the system, he's blamed the doctors and so-called therapists. He's severed all his connections to the entertainment world, and he's been trying to get her to do the same, clinging to the belief that once she's freed from the industry they can reunite. It's a ridiculous task. Sisyphean. Because no matter what, the woman he believes he knows was created from an Adam's rib in a studio office in Culver City.

Frank Sinatra waits in the private driveway to the right of the casino, proud owner of the Cal Neva Lodge, there to greet his guests and apologize for needing to run off so quickly. He kisses Pat on the cheek and drapes an arm around Peter's shoulder. Tonight after his show, he says, they'll all catch up. Shoot the breeze. He laughs, telling Pat that he'll be giving her a bit of advice for her brother. Frank then sends the Lawfords off with a bellhop, leaving him alone with Marilyn. He says he'll come by her cottage later; he wants to know how she's doing, talk more about this bullshit lawsuit from the studio. Her mind goes numb when people talk about the suit, as if it's being waged against someone else. Frank says something about it again, wants to make sure her lawyers are hitting back. Marilyn's too distracted by Joe watching, imagining him shaking his head, disgusted by the company she's keeping and knowing she'll never shed this character as long as she keeps herself as a part of the cast.

After Frank leaves, she turns her back to the hill, following the concierge toward her tan lake-view cottage, number three. He talks nervously, explaining that Mr. Sinatra needs to run the band through a rehearsal for the evening show in the Celebrity Room, and that she should have time to just relax for the next hour or so. But she's not listening. It's hard to hear anything with that stare burning into her back.

3:15 PM

She's kept the curtains half open, leaving a partial view of the lake. The cabin's almost dark. And smells of it, all closed up and stale with the scent of the shut-in. When she followed the concierge into the cabin, she looked once over her shoulder toward the hill. She couldn't see Joe. Couldn't even see the hill. But she can still feel him watching. His disappointment and hurt stream down the slope.

The bedsprings are tight. They barely give. She's on her back, her shirt bunched up at the bottom of her ribs, sinking into the red comforter. In the high altitude, her heart pounds hard, like it's trying to nail her into the round mattress. She closes her eyes, imagining Marilyn fading.

She sits up when she hears a knock on the door. "You can just leave it," she calls out. "Whatever it is." Her voice doesn't seem to carry. Her mouth is dry. So she tries again. "On the doorstep."

The knocking won't stop. She stands, tugs down her blouse, and then moves in small steps, arms straight at her sides.

Frank waits in the doorway, a bottle of Dom Pérignon tucked into his side, two glasses in his hand. "Room service," he says, deadpan, but unable to hold back a smile. There's a red napkin knotted around the neck of the bottle. His stance and expression come right from his stage show.

She's squinting, trying to bring him into focus. The vista behind him barely has shape. Like looking through someone else's prescription lenses.

"And let me really see you now," he says, pushing his way past her into the cabin. He leaves the bottle and glasses on the rattan desk in front of the window and yanks the curtains open all the way, spotlighting her. He steps in front of her, slight, his shoulders and hips still boyish. His size is in his swagger and confidence. But the showy demeanor disappears. Face to face with her, his presence withdraws, tightens. "Let me really get a good look at you," he says.

"No, look at that lake," she says, peering past him. "Now that'll cure the meanest of blues."

"I can tell you've come to the right place, because you look tired. Lousy with what the business has been giving you these days."

His impression surprises her. She hasn't seen herself as lousy. In fact, other than being a little tired, she's imagined herself looking spry, despite the implications from the studio about her age. Marilyn hugs her arms around her torso. She sways her hips and drops her head back. She wants to say, *really?* But instead goes into what's become a routine monologue about the new movie production and the lawsuit from Twentieth Century-Fox, about how they'd got her for nearly nothing on this crummy picture and then went and worked themselves up over anything she did, when everybody knew she was just another commodity. She says, "I tell those sons of bitches at Fox *good riddance*, and you know what they do, Frank? Hire me back and give me two more pictures. Forever their hostage. I should've been done with them, Frank. Finished."

"Well, now that you're here, you won't need to be falling apart over this nonsense. It doesn't exist in my house."

Does she really look as though she's about to fall apart? She's tempted to ask, but isn't that the way both her mother and grandmother reacted when met with similar inquiries? As though everyone else was the crazy one. "No need to worry," she reassures, although she hates how easily she slipped back into Marilyn's world with almost no prompting. Her eyes scrunch, almost impish, looking over to the champagne bottle. "Let's drink to my health. A toast to a weekend of making right."

He twists off the cork. There's barely a pop. Pouring a glass for each of them, he says, "Now that's a toast I can drink to."

He wipes his mouth with the back of his sleeve.

She says, "Pour me another."

Sitting on the edge of the bed, he leans over to the desk without lifting himself up and grabs the bottle. She's square in the center atop the comforter, her back straight, legs crossed Indian style. Her arm is stretched out, holding the empty glass.

He says his people tell him that DiMaggio is staying at the Biltmore across the street, but if she's concerned about it she needn't be, because Joe will not be allowed into the Cal Neva. She tells him Joe's okay, that he can just be a little—but Frank interrupts and says this is about a breach of friendship, ever since Joe started publicly blaming Frank and others for her troubles. He says, "This is not about you, even though it's all about you." She doesn't say she saw Joe on the hill.

Frank fills both their flutes and, not paying attention, sets the bottle down partially on the base of a lamp, and as it tilts to the side, the red kerchief slips off, landing on the arm of the desk chair, stuck on the rattan weave. He stretches back across to prop the bottle up, but only after he's watched a little bit of the champagne spill, enough of a stream to trickle off the desktop.

She says there's something she needs to ask him, and he tells her anything, and she says, no, she's really serious. This is serious. "So ask me," he says. "Ask me something serious."

She clears her throat while reaching for words, saying that for this weekend she just needs as much of a break from *her* showbiz world as possible. And she asks, "Do you think that's possible? Is it *really* possible?"

"That's why I invited you."

"I know, Frank," she says. "I know. It's only that . . ." She stops. "Oh, never mind. Forget I even said anything."

He just nods, knowing you break the silence only if you think you can make it better.

Before he leaves, Sinatra has Marilyn promise that she'll come to the evening show. He doesn't want her concerns to get in the way of a good time. He tells her just to sit in the back and enjoy. That's why she's here, to relax and have a good time. He reiterates that there is zero for her to worry about. This is a community he's built for his friends. There will be no clown show on his turf. On that she has his word. Now, to get to the Celebrity Room, he reminds her, she can just take the tunnel that runs from his cabin closet. No one will bother her that way. Follow it right to the show room. No detours. Straight through. "And remember," he says, "you've given me your word that you'll be there."

She picks the red kerchief off the chair and waves it like a surrender flag. "I said *promise*, didn't I? Believe me, I wouldn't miss it for the world."

Sinatra paces the short length of the cottage. He stops at the window, looking out. The afternoon sun is blinding off the lake. He shakes his head. Picks at something behind his right earlobe. "You know," he says, before turning around, "I do believe this change of scenery is going to do you good."

1956

The actor Eli Wallach often tells the story of walking down the street in New York with Marilyn and suddenly realizing that nobody recognizes her. How strange that was. Even for New York. But when he mentions it to her, she tells him it isn't strange at all; she is only noticed when she wants to be, and, as an offer of proof, she stops and says to watch this. She takes a deep breath, rolls her neck, and shakes out her arms and hands. Pushes at her hair. And then starts walking again. The tone of her skin softens. Her hips sashay. The blond in her hair takes on an unreal sheen. Her lips, half-open, deepen into a blood red. And, as if from an animator's hand, her whole figure seems to mold into an exaggerated shape and glow almost celestially. Within seconds she's surrounded. People point from across the street. Cameras are fumbled for and aimed. Taxis slow down, their passengers pushed against the windows, cupping their hands against the glass.

Later she'll say that sometimes the mood to become Marilyn can just hit. But usually it will last only for a moment.

Spring 1956: The Actors Studio, New York City

In a café on Ninth Avenue, just around the corner from the Actors Studio on West Forty-Fourth Street, she sits in the corner, disguised with a black wig and horn-rimmed glasses, looking like something a casting director might have imagined to be her bookish twin sister. On her lap rests a copy of *Anna Karenina*. On the table, a demitasse of espresso, barely touched. A quiet space. One that allows for thought. A place, she says to herself, where Marilyn Monroe would never dream of being. She's at the end of part three of the novel, having just reached the point where Alexei Karenin refuses to grant Anna a separation, insisting she stop her affair with Count Vronsky and return to a normal life. She plans to take a break as soon as she finishes the section. But she knows when she picks it up again, she will do as she always does, return to page one and re-read the opening sentence: *Happy families are all alike; every unhappy family is unhappy in its own way.* If Tolstoy had been allowed only one sentence to write his novel, that would've been enough for her. The pause at the semicolon. That's where she wants to be. In that space between clauses, because she's lived both versions of those families—happy and unhappy. Over the past months, she's reread the opening sentence over and over, trying to dig at it the way a soldier digs out his foxhole, readying herself to burrow in for survival.

The last time she checked in to Westside Hospital to calm her nerves, she decided to make some changes, and one of the changes was in how she'd let herself be treated. She hadn't wanted to be around people who acted like she was dumb. She told that to a nurse, and the nurse said, "Honey, don't waste your time fretting. All the smarts in the world couldn't have thought you up."

She slips into Lee Strasberg's class at the Actors Studio at the last possible minute. Rows of folding chairs fill the core of the former church. They face the stage, ringed by an empty balcony. Taking a place near the back, she tries to keep her stare down, avoiding eye contact, knowing some people will be looking at her. She doesn't want to intrude. She wears a scarf over her head and hides her body under a baggy black cardigan, its hem hanging well below her waist. Her legs are crossed, almost tangled, while her arms press hard against her chest, hiding any hint of her breasts. It's as though her body has folded in, trying to disappear within itself. Quickly, she darts a glance, taking inventory of the faces. At least thirty fellow students. All look sophisticated. Focused. Impassioned. Even the young ones have a certain wear on their faces. A sense of bravado and desire etched in, what she thinks of as "character." They appear comfortable sitting there. As though they know they belong. Surely, many of them have been on stage before. She's never even seen a play. Already she's envious. She wants what they have. But here's the irony that she knows and keeps to herself: despite all their artistic ambitions and pretensions, they'd almost all rather be her.

She wiggles her toes, trying to keep her foot from falling asleep.

Mr. Strasberg takes the stage, pulling up a director's chair and sitting. He leans back, relaxed and slouching, his elbows resting on the wooden arms. In his black suit, he almost disappears into the scrim. One sock scrunches down, a bare shin visible below the pant cuff. Still, his posture is confident. His body wide open. Today, he begins, he would like to remind everybody that theater is a creative art, and just because it uses a script, that does not make it an interpretative art. He peers at the group through his thick-framed glasses. Your art, he continues, demands a fresh, original, spontaneous experience with what you're dealing with, not an imitation of someone else's experience. He thrusts his hands out, then pulls them back in, folding them over his heart. And, he continues, what you will all be challenged with as creative actors is how to consciously stimulate the creative process, which usually takes place unconsciously. We want you as actors to stimulate your entire being beyond the external means of voice, gestures, speech. You will stimulate it with your own thoughts, sensations, sensitivities, experiences, and emotions— you will fuse completely with the life that has to be created on the stage. Or another way of thinking about it: when something is happening to the character, *something* is happening to the actor.

She moves to the edge of the chair, her arms now unfolded, rubbing her knee with the heel of her palm. She has let herself be constructed like one of those brilliant back-lot sets, where the façade is as lifelike and elegant and perfect as one can imagine, but to walk behind it is to see plywood sheets and two-by-four braces. She needs to remember that she is not that façade, no matter how much she has allowed herself to be built that way.

Strasberg stands near the conclusion of his lecture. The next class will be a series of scenes to be workshopped. He points out two students, who purse their lips and nod affirmatively. She can't imagine standing on the stage in front of all these people.

There's still too much to learn. But it doesn't bother her, not being ready. For once, she doesn't feel as if she's in any hurry.

She likes the smell of New York. The way it smells of the street, carried low and thick, trapped between buildings, rising from the subway vents. It's the smell of ideas, of commitments. The smell of frustration and sweat. And she finds it inspiring. It reminds her to work harder. To remember that ideas need roots. That they're not all dandelion clocks, immediately scattered into the horizon by the breath that just spoke them.

It's funny how a place can feel like home. And though she's been a Southern California girl her whole life, in many respects the epitome of it, New York feels like the place she was supposed to be born into. And she considers buying a house in Brooklyn. Imagines never going back to California again. And what was something of an ongoing flirtation with Arthur Miller for several years has turned serious. They see each other regularly. Trying to keep it quiet. Not make an issue of it. They read together. Talk. Bicycle in Central Park. On the Ocean Parkway in Brooklyn. And she loves that he recognizes that she has a New York soul. That he wants to nurture it. Refine it. And she thinks he might be the first *real* man Marilyn Monroe has ever known.

It's an idea Lee Strasberg has, and it's all his. He sits with her and some other students in Childs Restaurant. Square in the middle. He leans in to Marilyn, telling her that he's serious, it is the role for her. And she says it's impossible to hear anything, between all the chatter and the sizzling grill, not to mention the way the sound bounces off the white tiles. Again, he repeats, it's *the role* for her. "Tell me, Mr. Strasberg," she says, moving in. "Tell me the role for me."

He scoots even closer, his lips almost touching her ear. "Lady Macbeth," he says. "Lady Macbeth."

"Lady Macbeth?"

"Lady Macbeth."

She drums her fingers on the table. Pulls away, and looks at him. Smiling and shaking her head. "Oh, come on now," she says. "I haven't even done a scene in the lab."

"But you will be ready." Already it's hard for him to keep it in, so much so that others at the table ask what's going on. Strasberg blurts it out. And, looking right at Ben Gazzara, who's taking a bite of his sandwich, Strasberg says he should play Macbeth. He doesn't even notice that Gazzara, with his mouth full, nearly chokes.

But Marilyn does. She's aware of how ludicrous this all sounds, and the impression it leaves at the table. Since she first arrived, the suspicion that Lee Strasberg would find any way to make use of her reputation has been whispered between classes, never fully hushed when Marilyn walks by. In Childs Restaurant, cramped between her colleagues, she tries to force a smile, one that shows the ridiculousness of the idea, making sure all can see, shaking her head and rolling her eyes. It's hard for her to pull off convincingly. While she knows she's nowhere near ready for that kind of role, and that the idea truly is silly, she does want to believe she could play Lady Macbeth in the near future. She wants to believe that maybe this is the life she was meant to lead.

When they talk privately, Strasberg continues to reinforce the idea that it's all there inside her, every emotion it takes to make a role real. She's lived it all. Felt it. All those painful years of her childhood were not a pure waste. He just needs to get her to the point where she can access those memories, and teach them how to become her characters. He says he knows it's there. Her core is a gift. A talent. One that can't be taught, only coached. And, if she'll learn, she'll be able to play any role. *Any role.* And she asks, "Do you really think Lady Macbeth?" and he answers, "Any role."

To hasten the process and the training, Strasberg sets Marilyn up to see a psychiatrist to help her dredge through all of that past. He explains that Marianne Kris, whose office is in his building, is a true Freudian, in fact a very close friend of Anna Freud. Dr. Kris's father was not only a collaborator with Sigmund Freud, he also served as the pediatrician to the Freud family.

In short, Dr. Kris truly understands the science of re-pressed emotions, and its relationship to making art.

Together, acting as a family, he says, they will be able to undo what Hollywood has done.

Spring 1956: Central Park West, New York City

You sit on the couch. Sometimes more than twice a week. Sometimes daily. In a typically dark paneled room, you feel equally dark, only defined as a penumbra. And the therapist asks you how you're feeling. She checks her notes, bringing them under the light. How is the *sense of loneliness* today? There's a pause. You hear the ticking clock. It punches at you. And you try not to smile. A bus roars by beneath the window. Once you answer her with a degree of confidence and positivity (*Actually, I'm doing okay today*), and she says something about masks and subterfuges, and that sometimes when we don't feel lonely we are, in fact, at our loneliest.

She calls you Marilyn (*Well, Marilyn; So, Marilyn; And . . . Marilyn*). Today she says it's important to confront another piece of the past. And you say, "Where should we start?" and she answers, "Well, Marilyn, where would you like to start?" And you want to say, *Some pills would be good*, but it might be misconstrued, and not be taken for a laugh but instead as one more scribble on the notepad, a subject for future discussion. And she's just looking at you, pushing the top of her pen against her lips, denting them white, while her crossed stockinged legs never move, as though they've been lacquered shut. And before she can say, *Well, Marilyn* again, you lean forward, pushing your hands into the cushions, and you say, "That's kind of difficult, you know?" and she pushes the pen even harder into her lower lip, and then says, "I don't know. Perhaps you'll explain it to me, Marilyn."

And here's where you're caught, in a kind of vast no-man's-land set between definable borders. And you live there, sort of like a visitor who's read the brochures, a tourist who knows more of the facts and the histories than the actual residents do but has no real claim to firsthand experience. And you're tempted to use that metaphor, but you're lousy at metaphors (night classes at UCLA may have given you the appreciation but not the ability), and what you ought to say is that if the doctor is trying to get you to talk about Norma Jeane, then you can without a doubt talk about Norma Jeane. Aren't you her biographer, for God's sake? You can rattle off the series of foster homes, stays with relatives, and the way the world turned a blind eye to her, making her want to be seen all the more. You can detail it. Perform it. Make it truer than it was. But now it's nothing more than that. Norma Jeane was ended years ago. You might even say that, if you didn't know the knee-jerk response would be, "And how does that make you feel?" to which you'd have to reply, "You should ask Norma Jeane." And that kind of response, it seems, would get you nowhere.

One time you intimated that Norma Jeane had been ended on a specific day. It just kind of slipped out when you were going on about what it felt like the first time you modeled in front of the camera, on your lunch break at the Radioplane factory. And you talked about how you'd felt your entire body kind of cracking open in front of the lens, but it wasn't a breaking sensation, instead one that oozed. And you slipped into a metaphor by saying it was as though you were seeing color for the first time, and that, in a weird way, you sort of saw yourself three-dimensionally, the way others began to see you, specifically the factory men who suddenly went big eyed and insisted on walking you to your car and stared at your chest beneath a sweater too small for you while sweet-talking you from all angles. That day, posing before the camera, you saw her too. And along with the factory men, you too wanted to walk her to her car. Make sweet-talk and check out her body. That was the day, you let it slip, when Norma Jeane was ended. "Now we're getting to the place where we want to be," the doctor said. And you looked at her with utter confidence and assurance, as though the roles had been switched, and said, "No we're not. Not at all."

Ulysses
> *Leaves of Grass*
> *Madame Bovary*
> *Notes from Underground*
> *Paradise Lost*
> *The Prophet*
> *Death in Venice*
> *Swann's Way*
> *Anna Karenina . . .*

She stops you there. But your mind is racing, trying to picture the bookshelf, the nightstand, and the syllabus. She leans forward, legs still crossed. She draws in a breath through her nose that is startlingly loud. "This is my question," she begins. Her hands are clasped, the right is massaging the left. "Do you think," she asks, "that your purpose for reading all these books, for taking the night classes at UCLA, is, in part, a way for Norma Jeane to prove or to demonstrate that she can rise above her upbringing?" There's a temptation to challenge the fallacy of the question, that there's even a Norma Jeane that exists to prove anything. Or that Norma Jeane could ever rise above her upbringing, because in fact she can't, she ended (or was ended). But that kind of talk sounds too crazy, even for a therapist's office, and so you just shake your head. "No," you reply, "I just really like to read."

She seems interested in you. She even seems to like you. Maybe that's why you keep coming back? And at first it was supposed to be about your acting and training. A way to touch all the emotions inside you. Wade through the damage. Remember what it all felt like. And there always seemed to be a slight contradiction, in that it never quite made sense actually to heal any of the past, because that pain was the very thing you needed to draw on. This process has seemed to be more about locating and accessing. But as you've continued, and she identifies this central theme of loneliness, she's altered the plan, because she honestly thinks she can fix you. She wants to make it all go away. She doesn't want you to access it. She wants you to come to terms with it. Then it will have no power over you. Lose its effect. And though it's tempting, that's not quite what you signed up for. This was supposed to be about acting. Plus, and more importantly, if she actually opened you up, scooped out all the muck, then you know where you'd end up—at Norwalk State Hospital, taking your place in the line of women who came before you. No question. So you have to keep it controlled. End the things that need to be ended. And make sure there isn't really a past. Just a few biographical details, and some residual emotions to bring before the camera. Still, you like having someone who cares. Someone who seems to really want to help you, and not just take from you. And so you keep the appointments. Always show up on time. Give just enough to make it seem real. And, in a way, kind of look forward to it. Because it's nice to know there's a person who wants to hear what you have to say, and is interested in it. And because of that trust, you try to be mindful that even if the things you say aren't always entirely factual, they're always truthful.

"Sex," she says. "Should we talk about sex?"

"Do we have to?"

"Does that make you uncomfortable?"

"Sex!?"

"No," she says with a smile (betraying what's always supposed to be a professionally stone-faced expression). "I meant talking about it."

But what is there to say? You've always felt sexual. Even as a little girl. Your sexuality has been an essence of your being for as long as you can remember, as much a part of you as any other bodily function. But maybe the mistake you've made is to confuse it with sex, and that always seems to be a little disappointing because you realize that fucking (*is it okay to use that word?*) really bears little relationship to expressing the sexuality that you feel within yourself. And maybe that's because the feeling is so personal, and while over the years all these boys and men who've seen your sexuality have tried to get to it, to touch it, to own it, in a strange way it's as though having sex is the very moment when your sexuality completely turns itself off. It may be crude to say, but you understand how a whore can take it day in and day out without feeling a thing.

She asks, "Would you describe this as a fear of intimacy?"

"No," you say. "Maybe a fear of having no intimacy."

"I want to get back to that idea about 'the whore.'"

"I thought you might."

"I'm wondering if you're telling me that having sexual relations makes you feel like a prostitute?"

"Not at all."

"Perhaps you can clarify. For my benefit."

You lean back on the couch. The room is tightening. Suddenly it takes all your effort to sit still. Didn't you indicate you really didn't want to talk about this when she brought it up? Isn't this really her entrée into a discussion about repression? About your cousin Buddy feeling you up when you were living in his house? Old Man Goddard playing grab-ass? The boys at school? The slow march into the diagnosis that you've shut yourself down sexually in order to protect yourself from those painful memories? But again (and this is what you can't say), this is not an *issue*. Those all went with Norma Jeane. And you have no objection to borrowing those emotions if they will help with a future role. But the doctor's looking at you as though she expects you to talk, and so you'll tell her a story that a photographer once told you. That as a side project, an art project, he was taking pictures of whores along the Tijuana border. And in a motel room, he asked one of the women if he could shoot her just on the bottom sheet, since, up to that point, she would pose only on top of the covers. And she looked at him. Stiffened. Shook her head. And actually wagged her finger. *No*, the whore had said. *Above the sheet is for the customers. Underneath the sheet is for me.*

Marilyn. She keeps saying that name. (*Marilyn. Marilyn. Marilyn. Marilyn. Marilyn.*) She says, "Marilyn, we mustn't lose sight of why you're here. We want to alleviate those feelings of loneliness. Find ways to control and mitigate those moments of desperation that are liable to drop in on you unexpectedly. And to that end we need to focus on the triggers, Marilyn. What are those triggers, be they issues of abandonment or sexual assault, that are lying like mines waiting to explode inside of you? And how can you learn not to fear them? It's about developing the tools to accept them."

"That last one's not a question, is it?"

"What I'm saying is that we have to get inside. Continue to go deep into Marilyn, and root out those elements of her past."

You're careful not to smile. You don't want to offend, because, again, you kind of like her, and you like that she likes you. But it does make you want to smile every time she talks about Marilyn and Marilyn's past. Maybe it's because Marilyn's past is no more than a few years old? Maybe because there are entire payrolls dedicated to making Marilyn's past? Or that that past is a work-in-progress being created on a regular basis in *this* very office? And that just like Norma Jeane, at some point in the not-too-distant future, you predict, Marilyn will cease to exist, and with her will go all that past?

When you first came to New York, you used the pseudonym Zelda Zonk to avoid attention when making reservations. It isn't difficult to imagine sitting in this office in a few years, digging at the dirt, trying to pull up the roots of Zelda's past, listening to Zelda Zonk being reminded that when we don't feel lonely we are, in fact, at our loneliest.

Spring 1956: The Actors Studio, New York City

She'll be doing her first scene at the Actors Studio in less than an hour. She waits alongside the stage, trying not to let the anticipation get the better of her. The piece is from Eugene O'Neill's play *Anna Christie*, a two-person scene, in which she's cast as Anna Christie opposite Maureen Stapleton's Marthy Owen. As he always does, Mr. Strasberg continues to emphasize that the scene, as with all those at the Studio lab, is about process and experimentation, and that it should not be thought of as "performing" or "auditioning"—the lab is a "protected environment." Still, she feels the eyes of critics studying her. And while she knows some of them might be curious to see how much she's really learned, she suspects most want to confirm she's learned nothing at all.

Maureen comes up to her. She also looks nervous. She's shorter than Marilyn, but somehow Marilyn looks more diminutive. Maureen's is a solid physique, one that already has cast itself as the stalwart, balanced by a contrasting vulnerability that resides in her cherublike face. "Almost ready," Maureen says, not quite a question. Her feet dance in place.

"Almost ready."

Over the past few weeks, they have not been able to rehearse the scene without Marilyn making a mistake. But that hasn't been due to an inability to understand the character or the context. She's studied the play nightly. Discussed it with her classmate, Jeannie Carmen, over coffee at corner cafés. Made it the focus of evening conversation with Arthur at the apartment on Sutton Place, where they've taken it apart both structurally and thematically, and even run through other scenes from the play, with him taking on the role of Old Chris. It was only when she rehearsed at the studio that she couldn't remember her lines. Maureen suggested some old acting tricks, either writing out all the lines by hand or just leaving an open script on a table on the stage. Marilyn didn't know what would work. In truth, when it was quiet, when she was alone and not picturing anything, she knew the script inside out. The words came into her head, rich and lyrical, as though she were listening to somebody else's recitation. It was only when she thought about it. Pictured herself onstage. Hearing her naysayers lean over each other to whisper *The stage is not the movies.* That was when she lost them.

She and Maureen have done everything to keep this scene from becoming a spectacle—including changing dates, writing fake names on the schedule—but as the room begins to fill with people who typically never attend the lab workshops, it becomes clear this will be the circus they've been hoping to avoid. "Sometimes," Maureen says to Marilyn, "you just get a bad case of the nerves right before you go on." She isn't really conversing; she's just talking. Almost chattering. "They're buried in your body. Deep inside. Where the bones rattle. But then it's as if the nervousness just pops as soon as the curtain rises. Like a bubble. Gone. And then you float right through."

Marilyn doesn't say anything. She can only nod. Usually she just defaults to her menu of pills, any one of them made to level her anxiety. But she's resisted the impulse; experience tells her that the necessary dosage for this level of nerves would only disorient her. She adjusts the belt of the tan raincoat she picked for the scene, tightens it, and tries to steady her breath. Maureen's tension only makes her more nervous. Reaching into the coat pocket, Marilyn mumbles, "I brought this," covertly pulling out a fifth of Jack Daniels. "Just in case, like me, you don't take your coffee black."

Almost all the seats are taken. The level of chitchat rises and echoes up with the leftover prayers into the old church rafters.

The two women stand together, sipping their coffee and whiskey. Given the chance, they would wait forever.

Strasberg's voice cuts through the room's din. Then the house quiets.

Maureen says, "Okay, I guess we're just about on."

"Then we'd better take our places."

"Yes, we better."

"Maureen," Marilyn says.

"Yes?"

"I know them."

"You know them."

"My lines."

It's a relief when the scene ends. Strasberg already is calling out that it was terrific. Extending his arms. Standing up. Clapping his hands. But she doesn't feel it. And though she knows she isn't supposed to think of the scene as an audition or performance (just a "protected environment"), she's aware that Lady Macbeth has slipped that much further away.

When she walked onstage, Marilyn became aware of her steps being too heavy. Her feet felt like they thudded the boards, making it almost physically impossible to reach Maureen. She worked to compensate. Tried to lighten her exterior. Bring an added delicacy to her movements. A controlled hush to her speech. By the end, though, she wasn't sure she ever found the control. But at least no lines were dropped.

She and Maureen step into a shadowed area, away from Mr. Strasberg. Away from everybody. On the stage, it was as though they were nothing more than two people occupying a single space, jabbering alternately between pauses. Now they're like strangers who have endured a common disaster, forever connected by the shared experience. They try to congratulate each other, laughing at how a collision of nerves can only result in an implosion. Marilyn says she's going to return the Jack Daniels, claiming it was clearly a defective brew. They take each other's hands and then let them drop. Turning to leave, they simultaneously wipe their palms on their respective hips.

When she returns to Hollywood, they will talk and talk about her New York ways and her so-called method acting, trying to bend her back into their premade Hollywood shape, and then get furious when they discover she is not that pliable. Some will accuse her of a newfound pretension. But she'll be focused in a way she's never been before.

Spring 1956: Los Angeles

Arthur is afraid of what his association might do to her career. Joe McCarthy's committee has been breathing down his neck, promising a subpoena that will compel him to name his friends in order to save his reputation and livelihood—not to mention save himself from going to jail.

He could just stay in the desert forever, he says to her over the telephone from the phone booth at Pyramid Lake. She's in Los Angeles shooting *Bus Stop*, awaiting the summary divorce that will be awarded to him after the mandatory six weeks it takes to become a Nevada resident. Then they'll marry. But maybe he just won't come out of the desert, he says. There are cowboys he's met who live in holes in the desert, he tells her, and unless you know exactly where those holes are, you'll never have a chance at finding those men. All completely off the grid. They come up only when there's a chance for work. "I could do that," he says. "Only you'd have the map of where to find me."

"Don't be silly," she replies. "You're from Brooklyn. You're not going to live in a hole in the Nevada desert."

"Have you ever imagined what it would be like to live totally outside the mainstream?"

She thinks of Norwalk State Hospital, where the long white hallways feel like fault lines off which the private rooms splinter.

Ignoring his question, she tells Arthur time isn't passing fast enough, and that she can't wait until the Reno divorce kicks in and they can be together again. He replies that at least being out in the desert is inspiring him to write. Maybe he'll end up writing something for her. Maybe a picture. "How about we get through the next six weeks," she says, "without the FBI getting another new thing to dig up?"

"How about it," he says.

"How about it."

Because he loves her that much, he went to Nevada for the divorce, renting a cabin at Pyramid Lake sight unseen. The area, a terrain of flat valleys and low hills buttressed by dried lakes, a thousand years of geologic coincidence, is as different as possible from anything he ever knew growing up among tenement buildings that crowded the sidewalks. A desert allegedly guarded by poisonous snakes hidden in wait, ready to snap at the scent of a threat. And he had to walk vigilantly around the Pyramid Lake shoreline, keeping watch for quicksand. Apparently there were warning signs posted at one time, but they kept disappearing, and the county became weary of replacing them. Some figure the signs were just taken under by quicksand. Others accuse the Paiutes of stealing them in the night, with the idea that it would take only one or two fisherman being sucked under to ward off future poachers from this sacred area, though that seems a little far-fetched, aside from the fact that, on the rare occasion, rotted bodies have been spotted bubbling up to the surface, before being vacuumed under again just as quickly.

Because he loves her that much, he went to Nevada for the divorce.

That's how much he loves her. And that love makes her love him back. Even more.

Going up Century Boulevard to the studio, Marilyn senses she's being tailed. At the gates, where the guard checks her name off the clipboard, she hears shutters clicking. She can feel binoculars zooming in on her as she scoots into her trailer on the back lot. Once inside, she draws the shades. The room changes to sepia. The sun beats down on the studio back lot while the cool Pacific air blows up Century Boulevard, creeping under the doorjamb. Being back in LA drains her. In only a matter of months, she grew used to the pace of New York, to the different expectation of craft and dedication. Even with Paula Strasberg here to coach her while she's shooting *Bus Stop*, Marilyn still feels in between. Going backward and forward at the same time. She sits on a cushioned bench, then slumps, resting her head on the card table, the vinyl sticking to her cheek. She shades her face with her palm and reminds herself that if she needs to talk she's supposed to talk in whispers. The bugging devices aren't that good.

She calls him in Nevada at nine o'clock at night, from a pay phone on Sunset—just in case. Put on hold, she continues to drop coins into the slot, feeling shaky for the ten minutes it takes for Arthur to come to the phone. She leans against the side of the booth, her mouth practically touching the fingerprinted glass wall. When he finally gets on, her voice is trembling. She wonders what took so long. Arthur reminds her that she's called him at a phone booth that is down the road from his cabin and that it was the landlord who answered and then went to get him. It's a bit of a procedure, he says, going up and down the dirt road at

Pyramid Lake, especially in the dark of night. But it's what they have. She waits for him to pause, and then interjects that she can't handle it, and before he can say *handle what*, she says, "This crap of a moviemaking, and all the waiting," and she swears she won't have it anymore, and she feels like she's about to come crashing, and no one in her circle has the strength to keep her from shattering. He says he can come out in the morning, but then the six weeks will be broken, and they don't give you credit. They've got rules, the state of Nevada. He and Marilyn will have to start the wait all over again. Another six weeks.

She says, "We'll keep it quiet. We can meet somewhere in the valley. What are the chances? It's worth the risk."

He says it's a risk, but he'll think about it.

"That means you won't come, doesn't it?"

"No," he says. "It means I need to think about it. Figure it out."

"So you're coming?" She doesn't try to hide the excitement in her voice.

"I'm thinking on it."

The following afternoon he's in LA. It's safe for only an evening; he'll have to be gone by the following morning. Arthur tells her he decided to come because he's concerned about her, unable to admit that coming was also for him. But she lets him have that. They don't talk about committees or divorces or movie sets, and hardly of marriage. They mostly stay silent. A sense of surveillance still hovers. Together, she and Arthur sit in her room, number 41 at the Chateau Marmont, listening to a reel-to-reel tape of Mr. Strasberg that Paula dropped off, saying it had to be heard. On the recording, Mr. Strasberg lectures on the acting techniques of Eleanora Duse. His voice comes through the machine's speaker, clear and distinct; anybody eavesdropping through the walls would think it was he who lived there. Mr. Strasberg doesn't so much talk about Duse as pose questions about why she was so revered. There is authority in his tone, yet still Mr. Strasberg speaks with wonder; in a way it's like religion, the very sense of structure Marilyn sometimes craves. She rubs Arthur's thigh, occasionally glances over to him, looking for his reactions. She suspects that were she to stop the tape and ask him what Mr. Strasberg just said, Arthur wouldn't be able to answer. His expression never changes. And when she does stop the tape, and Mr. Strasberg's voice slows down and trails off, she senses Arthur snap awake. She says she's hungry. She suggests a café she knows up the street, as old-world European a place as one can find on the Sunset Strip, where the walls are papered in thick browns, and the lightbulbs glow a dingy yellow, and the air moves only when the front door opens. She asks, "Should we go now? Or did you want to hear the end of the lecture?" And the way in which he offers the choice back to her, despite his blatant lack of interest in Lee Strasberg's opinion about Eleanora Duse, makes her love him just a little bit more.

A moist evening air blows off a horizon that's starting to wilt into the haze. For the first time all week she doesn't think about being watched. They move up the strip without speaking, until they reach the European restaurant and are greeted at the door by a host named Henri who speaks to them only in French. The European restaurant is even more ridiculous than she made it sound, with its piped-in cabaret music and an interior meant to replicate a street café. But she doesn't say anything, other than how safe she feels to be there with him.

The restlessness returns the next morning, once he's gone. The car will be arriving shortly at the Chateau Marmont to take her to the set. She's already dressed, her hair tied back under a scarf. For once ahead of schedule. Paula Strasberg waits in the room next door. They agreed to meet out front when the car arrived.

She sits on the bed, smoothing out the wrinkles in the bedspread. Then turns on the radio, adjusting the volume to a whisper. And she faces the wall and tries to breathe in. Hoping to fill her chest. When he left, Arthur told her he would see about returning next week; meanwhile, they both need to focus on their work to get through this phase. She promised she would try to save her pills for when she really needs them.

They talk that night. She tells Arthur they don't need to worry. They'll make it through this waiting period.

And then they can move into a whole new life. It's not hard to start over, she assures him. Trust me. She says it into the phone, a hand cupped over the receiver, with her voice lowered and hushed, but speaking so quickly she can barely keep the words in order.

Midsummer 1956:
New York City & Washington, D.C.

Although she didn't want him to go to jail, she always encouraged Arthur not to cooperate with the committee, even if it meant contempt of Congress charges. The night before they left for Arthur's testimony in Washington, Spyros Skouras, the president of Twentieth Century-Fox, came by their apartment, hoping to convince Arthur to cooperate. He offered Arthur a way out, saying he could persuade some of the congressmen he had relationships with to relent if Arthur compromised by making a statement that thanked the committee for giving him the opportunity to realize he'd made mistakes, and to testify before Chairman Walter that he was glad for the chance to reconstitute his love for America, and was now fearful of people he'd once admired. She'd watched the whole thing from their bar, drinking scotch and running cognac out to Skouras.

Arthur fumed.

She understood full well that the only reason Skouras cared was because of her impending marriage to Arthur and the effect his political stance might have on the salability of Marilyn and her movies. Maybe Skouras understood he wasn't going to succeed, because he suddenly stopped talking, grabbed his coat, and let Arthur see him to the elevator. Alone, Marilyn poured herself another scotch. She sipped it quickly before Arthur returned. It burned all the way down. She poured another. Hoping for the same.

After his hearing, Arthur didn't say much to her. He and his lawyer, Joe Rauh, came back to the Rauhs' apartment, where Marilyn had spent the day with Joe's wife, Olie, sequestered, out of sight of the Washington, D.C., media, and away from what Arthur perceived as unnecessary pressure. Once they walked in, it was as though the hearing had never happened, as if it had been only an inconvenience preceding her and Arthur's upcoming trip to England at the end of the week. What Marilyn did glean of the committee hearing was indirect—interrogations about petitions Arthur had signed, the rights of Ezra Pound to write his poetry, and his invocation of the Fifth Amendment when asked to confirm the Communist leanings of fellow writers. The only thing concrete was when Joe Rauh laughed, saying how this all could've been avoided if Arthur had just allowed Marilyn into the Capitol to pose for photos with Chairman Walter. But she was glad Arthur wasn't laughing. Even more glad he would never concede the fight. He burned so much energy trying to protect her from his battles, was so busy looking out for her that he hadn't stopped to notice how hard she'd been cheering. Like a fanatic sitting ringside, yelling, *Hit him again, put him down for good.*

Midsummer 1956: 2 Sutton Place, New York City

Rabbi Goldburg wants to meet with you on his own, commuting from Congregation Mishkan Israel in New Haven down to your Sutton Place apartment. At your front door, on the eighth floor, he stands, slightly winded, a satchel in one hand and a stack of books cradled under his arm—*What Is a Jew?*, *History of the Jews*, *A Partisan Guide to the Jewish Problem*, and the Conversion Manual of the CCAR—the texts, you'll learn, that he requires anybody who wants to convert to read. You bring him tea, then settle in the living room, the rabbi on the couch and you in the brown armchair. The window is cracked open; the apartment gets stuffy in summer. He's looking at you, nodding with a faint smile, and it's impossible to guess how he sees you. It feels a bit like an audition, one for which you haven't been given a script, and it's not exactly clear how you're being measured. You've never sat one-on-one with a rabbi before, and your first impression is that his demeanor is more like that of a professional man than you might have imagined, all

business. You shift, uncrossing your legs, then crossing them again. Finally, you break the quiet. "Well,"
you say, "welcome." "Yes," he says, "welcome." And
you say, "Shall we get started?" He leans back, spreading his arms along the top of the couch back; they
span almost the entire length. He says he wants you
to be comfortable, that *we're just going to have a little
initial chat.* "So let's start with the most basic of questions," he begins. "Why do you want to convert?"
You straighten yourself up, this one you know, and
you explain it's because you're going to marry Arthur,
and he's, well, you know. Rabbi Goldburg considers,
then tells you that, traditionally, marriage can never
be considered as the sole reason for a conversion; the
true reason needs to be a compelling desire to have a
Jewish identity and to be part of a shared future, and
he wants to know what you understand of that desire.
Now *you're* nodding, sirens screaming as they round
the corner on East Fifty-Seventh Street, not quite sure
of how to answer, because you haven't really thought
about it in those terms. The rabbi must see your con-
fusion, because he walks back his question and says,
"Allow me to ask you this, Miss Monroe. What are you
converting from?" and you say, "From?" and he says,
"If you're converting, then you have to be going *from*
something *to* something." And you remember your
great-aunt Mrs. Martin taking you to her fundamen-
talist church in Compton, but you were only a child,
and it was something forced upon you, something you

never even accepted enough to reject. So you look at Rabbi Goldburg, patiently waiting for your response, and all you can do is answer with another question: "Can *nothing* be *something*?"

July 27, 1962
_____

Cal Neva Lodge, Crystal Bay, NV

In speaking of training Marilyn Monroe, Lee Strasberg said,
"Her past need not destroy her; it might yet become part of the
vocabulary and technique of a new art."

3:50 PM

Set in no particular order, plastic bottles, some clear and some green, line the desktop:

- *Nembutal*
- *Decadron phosphate*
- *Chloral hydrate*
- *Seconal*
- *Rx 80521*
- *Rx 80522*
- *Rx 13525*
- *Rx 13526* (Double quantity. She's not sure what these are, other than that some are from the Beverly Hills Schwab's Pharmacy and others from the Prescription Center on Wilshire.)

She replays the conversation with Frank. Turns it into a version that doesn't end with him walking out the door, still advising her to relax, and assuring her that everything will be smooth on his watch. A version in which she isn't so cautious and she just comes clean about her need to disappear for a while. Explaining how *The Misfits* had seemed as though it would be an escape from Marilyn Monroe, but just a year later here she is again, dumped back into her old self in this latest production, *Something's Got to Give*, with her old life (including Joe) falling into a regular pattern as though the time away was nothing more than an adolescent girl's sophomoric escapade. She should've told Frank that sometimes it feels like this is it—her last chance, because it's become near impossible to control Marilyn Monroe the way she used to—that she's becoming her. And how regardless of one's family history or stature, we're all prone to falling apart; all of us, at some moment, end up standing on an edge, unsure we can keep from toppling over, forced to deal with our fragility then and there. That's where she is. And she'd tell him that she read something in the paper about how a major earthquake could knock the earth off its axis, and while the earth would continue to spin just fine, as a result of the disaster, each day would be shortened by a little more than a millionth of a second, and how for nearly everybody that would mean nothing except for those for whom a millionth of a second means everything. And for her that one-millionth could tip the scales. In the replayed conversation, she says that's why she came up here, that disappearing even for a weekend might let her hold on to that millionth of a second. Riding the earth bareback, clutching the reins, trying to steer clear of even the slightest bump.

Glancing at the lake reminds her how small she is. The reminder that you're only a sliver of something larger than you could ever be.

4:50 PM

As she steps toward the railing, the door closes on its own behind her. She walks in a side step, working her way off the porch, feet never crossing over each other, her eyes fixed on the lake at all times. It looks a little greener through her sunglasses. Even when the porch curves, changing direction toward the lodge, she still watches Lake Tahoe. It's just a matter of twisting her body.

She'd like to go to the hill across the highway, just to the base, where the wildflowers grow. Maybe pick some poppies and bring them back to the cabin. Put them in a water glass. Bring new life into the room.

She steps off the porch onto the macadam, feeling the last wooden slat bend. The road is hard and solid. Blankets of flowers slope down to the lakeshore, sometimes hidden and shaded by manzanita and other shrubs, but mostly sharp and distinct. They look impossible to reach.

She can't even see the hill.

"Miss Monroe?"

A big man in dark slacks and a crisp short-sleeved shirt takes off his sunglasses. He sticks them in his breast pocket, leaving one silver temple hanging out. He says he works for the Cal Neva. His face is wide and flat. He smells of cigarettes. Personal security, he tells her, for Mr. Sinatra's guests.

"You're charged with watching over me?"

"In a manner of speaking."

"Frank's told you to make sure I'm safe?"

He asks, "Is everything okay?"

"Yes," she nods. "Just fine. It's all okay." Behind him is the lodge, the back side, where the Circle Bar comes out. She lowers her sunglasses, squinting. "I thought you could see the hill from here," she says.

"The hill?"

"The one across the street. I saw it when I came in."

"The hill across 28? You'd have to be around the side of the building to see it clearly. Almost in the front."

"Really? I could swear I saw it from my porch earlier."

He scans the grounds. On guard, almost as though anticipating something. "Nope," he says. "Just from the side."

She looks around, but there are no flowers that catch her interest. "Maybe you could help me up there. To the side, then. Just to look at the hill. I'd like to look at it. There's something I'm looking for."

"There might be people there."

"They seem to be everywhere. People."

He tells her okay, but in a way that seems to suggest it's against his better judgment. Stalling, he puts his sunglasses back on. He coughs into his hand, then wipes his palm against his pant leg. His understanding, he explains, was that she wasn't to be disturbed, but if this is what she wants . . .

She says she's not disturbed. And it's what she wants.

It was warm when she left Los Angeles this morning, but it's even a little hotter here. Still, the air feels tighter, a bit more brisk, as though cutting across her instead of enveloping her. The smell of the pines takes over, and when the breeze blows from the south she can smell the lake water, pure and clear, because, oddly enough, pure and clear has its own smell.

She feels as though she is a stalk, and her petals are waiting to fall.

She tilts her chin up, trying to gauge the wind. The right gust could take her down.

The giant Cal Neva parking lot extends to the road. And from there she can make out the crest of the hill.

The bodyguard was wrong. Nobody is out. She takes a few steps, thinking she sees flowers dotting the hill. She considers going forward, but then stops. "Do you see anyone up there?" she asks.

"On the hill?"

"Yes, in line with us."

He fingers the sunglasses down to the tip of his nose. Peers over the top. Scans. "No," he says. "I don't see anything. But even if there was something to see, I'm not sure I could. It's pretty far away."

"I saw something earlier. When I first arrived."

"The wind blows the trees around, bending them into funny positions. It can make you do a double take out of the corner of your eye."

She shakes her head. "No," she says. "I saw someone. A person." She stops herself. After what Frank said earlier, she doesn't want to let on that it was Joe.

"I don't know what to tell you. Maybe some gawker or photographer. I don't know. We've heard of people sometimes trying to take pictures from up there. But you don't have to worry. Even if there was someone there, you were too far away to be anything but a speck."

Joe is not there. But she did see him when she arrived. She's sure of it.

The man says he can send someone to take a look if she's worried or feels threatened, but really, he says, it looks all clear.

She tells him it's okay. Really she just wants to pick flowers. To make a bouquet, she tells him. She says she'd like California poppies, that it must be legal to pick them on the Nevada side. "Maybe you can just help me find some here on the grounds," she says.

"I can have some sent to your room."

"No," she says, "I prefer to pick them myself."

As they walk the perimeter of the parking lot looking under bushes at the ground cover, she glances back once, at the last possible point to see the hill. She senses movement behind a tree, near the crest where the pines curve naturally into a half smile. Maybe it's Joe. Maybe he's peering out momentarily, before darting back and hiding behind the tall, lumbering pine.

She's bent down on one knee. Leaned forward, crouching, and pulling back the branches of a manzanita tree, its red bark peeling and curling with each tug. The bodyguard waits behind, standing sideways. He's not paying attention to her. A hummingbird appears over the patch she's reaching for, buzzing and hovering in place for a moment. Its wings are beating, and its heart thumps, and it looks suspended in place, as though held up by an electric current. As soon as it notices her, the bird darts away.

One hand keeps hold of the manzanita branch while she reaches the other in, grabbing several poppy stalks near the roots and pulling until they snap. A scent releases, and though initially it's acrid, there's a cleanliness to it, not quite sweet, but not like something risen from dirt.

She pulls the flowers in close, pressing the full bouquet against her chest. She glances back at the bodyguard. A stem brushes against her cheek. She takes in only a slight whiff, getting mostly the soil, but it's as though she's inhaled the whole plant. And she can feel it filling her, washing through her veins, being pumped in and out of her heart, and it feels so right in her body, as though she's made of glass, but not fragile, instead delicately structured and clear and clean and transparent, and this is the feeling, this is the one she wants to hold forever.

Clear. Transparent. And without form.

Nothing but a speck in the crowd.

1957–1960

Excerpts from the United Artists Pressbook for *The Misfits*

"I want to survive," the actress earnestly says about herself. "I'm looking to the future. I want to be around for a long, long time, which means I mustn't stand still professionally. They want to label talent in Hollywood. You're this, or you're that! If I can possibly avoid it, I'm not going to allow whatever talent I have to be labeled like that."

EXPLOITATION CAMPAIGN
Horseback Bally:
Have a couple (the girl should be an attractive blonde) ride around town on a horseback. They carry a sign which reads: "WE'RE GOING TO SEE THE PICTURE THAT EXPLODES WITH LOVE. IT'S 'THE MISFITS'—NOW AT THE BIJOU!"

EXPLOITATION CAMPAIGN
Find MM's Double
There are many girls who think they resemble Marilyn Monroe, this decade's most outstanding screen personality. Stage a search for Marilyn Monroe's local "double" with announcement of contest in your lobby and newspaper. Winner and runner up to get the full treatment consisting of possible appearance in local TV show, picture and story in newspaper, dinner at a top restaurant, hair-do at beauty parlor and orchids from florist.

August 1957:
444 East Fifty-Seventh Street, New York City

He tells her he's been thinking about his short story "The Misfits," the one he wrote in the Nevada desert. They're sitting on the couch in the New York apartment. Marilyn holds a pillow against her stomach. The doctors assured her the meds have stanched any potential pain and that whatever she feels are imaginary symptoms; the explanations sounded logical, but still it feels as though a knife is jabbing through her uterus. She looks over to a lit candle. She thinks she smells something burning. But it's just part of the match gone to ember, that piece she dropped when she thought her fingers were going to be burned.

The story, he says, is something of a response, a way to find meaning in the landscape and the people who surrounded him. And he recalls Pyramid Lake, almost like a mirage amid the lunarscape. And then there was Reno, and the Mapes Hotel, and the main room of the Nevada Club, filled with fresh smoke and the slight lilt of booze, and slots lining the rows evenly, chest high, blocked off by men whose jackets were slung over stools, and women in sleeveless blouses, carefree and quietly pulling on the machines' arms—the whole dreary scene oddly miscast against the bright patterns of the carpet and the velvet saloon-era wallpaper.

He holds a hand out to her. She keeps her arms around the pillow on her belly but stretches her feet across his lap.

Arthur keeps talking. He says it was mostly the people he needed to write out of his system. The old, mangled rodeo riders whose broken bodies left them useless, living in holes in abandoned silver mines, who craved Hollywood magazines with Hollywood movie cowboys on the cover, never quite accepting that they themselves were the real thing; and career ranch hands trying to find a place in a modernizing world, refusing to give up the life and vowing to work only for pay, never for wages; and the six-week divorcées, who'd arrived looking for something they weren't sure of and were living out their lives expecting that something better must be around the next corner. It was a place where people struggled with all their will to fit in, but only found themselves more alienated.

"A little like Hollywood," she says.

"A little."

She knows this is leading toward something, and she hopes that he's not going to break his silence about the operation. After all, it could barely be characterized as a miscarriage, since the tubal pregnancy was discovered almost immediately. She hasn't said anything about it to him since, and he looks away when he must sense she's thinking about it. Most of his days are spent in his studio. When he comes out they always stay on the surface, as though they can walk on it forever. A regular pair of Jesus Christs.

Arthur says what he's getting at is that he's been drafting "The Misfits" into a screenplay. He's really trying to write it with her in mind. In fact, after the story ran in *Esquire*, several people told him that they could picture Marilyn playing Roslyn. That it suited her. An ideal role to free her from the typecasting, one that would showcase her interior and really bust up the empty-blonde image that people have refused to let go of.

And later, when she thinks back on that evening, she won't recall the sincerity in his voice, the way it shook as if he were presenting an uncertain gift, and how his neck muscles clenched tightly to keep him from looking away. Instead she'll remember the spider in the corner of the wall they were facing, and how they both noticed the movement at the same time, and how Arthur pulled a tissue out of the box on the end table, and how when he stood her feet fell to the floor, and how he walked over to the corner, perched on his tiptoes, and covered the spider with the crumpled tissue, and how just as he was about to smash the spider, instead he picked it up and stood there in the middle of the room, holding the spider trapped in the Kleenex, looking at her, unsure of what to do with it.

October 1959: Beverly Hills Hotel, Los Angeles

She's nervous with anticipation, waiting for Arthur to return, to hear if Arthur's convinced him to take the part. They're staying at a hotel on the coast, and she hasn't left the living room all day, limiting herself to one pill that's done nothing. Once Arthur finally comes through the door, she says, *Tell me everything.* Demands it. She wants to know what Clark Gable said. Did he say he'll do the picture? After Huston signed on to the movie, Arthur was brought out to Los Angeles to try to close the deal with Gable. She paces across the hotel room. Takes hold of the curtains. The light is bringing on a headache. She takes one last look in the direction of the Pacific—she's watched those waves her whole life, drifting out and then roaring right back. But the beach is almost eight miles away; it can't deliver any solace. She yanks the curtains shut with unexpected force.

Arthur tells her it went well. "Actually," he says, "better than well."

She says you wouldn't know by his face.

"It was just a lot," Arthur says. "In a way I'm not accustomed to."

"But he said yes?"

"It took a lot of convincing."

"So he agreed?"

"He said he thought it was supposed to be a Western, but that he realized it wasn't, and that he was confused and really didn't know what to make of it."

"What did you tell him?"

"I didn't know what to say. I got tongue-tied. I just kept looking at him, thinking that this man *is* Gay Langland, and wondering how I could make him understand that, Western or not."

She sits down on the sofa, then springs back up. She just wants the end of the story.

He continues, "I told him it was an Eastern Western, and he kind of laughed, and I got more flustered, saying it wasn't about good guys and bad guys, or the evil within the good guys, and all those various genre conventions, but that it was existential, about how the so-called meaninglessness in our lives takes us to where we end up. And to tell you the truth, Marilyn, I had to stop talking after a while, because I wasn't quite sure what I was talking about anymore."

Standing toe to toe with Arthur, she puts a hand on each of his shoulders. She draws in close to him, clenching her grip. Her stomach tightens. She forces herself to speak slowly, controlled. "Arthur," she says. "For God's sake, did he say yes?"

He looks at her, almost with the shame of the scolded. "Yes," he says. "He said he'd do it."

She yelps out with joy, and it's a true joy, an emotion that feels almost foreign. Her heart pounds, and she dances in place, her smile so big and lumbering that it blocks any tears. "I've worshiped Gable all my life," she says, throwing her arms around her husband. "I must have been ten or so when I first saw him in *San Francisco*, and only a few years later he captured my heart in *Gone with the Wind*. My whole life I've idolized him. This is the real dream. The real dream coming true."

"I told you, you deserve this."

She kisses him on the forehead, then goes back to the window. Parting the curtains, she peeks out, imagining she can see the surf. One small wave forming on the surface, battling several breakers, reshaping and refusing to be swallowed. It lifts and curls and thrusts and finally touches the shore.

Late July 1960: *The Misfits* Set/Harrah's Club, Reno

On the first shooting call with Gable in *The Misfits*, Marilyn reports to the set at Harrah's at 11:45 AM. With her are the following:

1. Arthur Miller (scriptwriter and husband)
2. Rupert Allan (agent)
3. Paula Strasberg (acting coach)

4. Sydney Guilaroff (hair stylist)
5. Whitey Snyder (makeup artist)
6. Agnes Flanagan (hairdresser)
7. Bunny Gardel (body makeup)
8. Evelyn Moriarty (stand-in)
9. Ralph Roberts (masseur)
10. May Reis (secretary)
11. Shirlee Strahm (wardrobe)
12. Gussie Wyler (seamstress)
13. Hazel Washington (personal maid)

She's anxious, but not the kind of anxious that debilitates her, the kind of anxious that pinches at her, that makes her feel as ordinary as her upbringing and makes her wonder how it is that she could possibly stand among such great talent. She's in her trailer, alone, parked on Virginia Street in front of Harrah's Club, where the first scene with Clark Gable will be shot. She sits with her knees drawn in to her chest, just in front of the wall unit air conditioner; it's the one place that really feels cool, because it's late July in Reno, and this time of year the heat pounds around the clock. She's told it's been upward of 100 degrees every day the past week, which explains why the trailer walls are hot to the touch, and why it's only the steadily manufactured air that brings any relief.

The scene will be simple. Short. It's set in the lounge at Harrah's, where Roslyn and Gable's character, Gay, along with their respective friends, Isabelle and Guido (played by Thelma Ritter and Eli Wallach), first

meet. A dog named Tom Dooley will act as the cata-
lyst that brings them all together. The lines were easily
memorized. A good scene to break the ice with. But the
thought of Gable makes her antsy, and for a split second
she imagines him wondering who she is, and why he's
acting opposite her. She just needs to prepare herself. It's
a mental thing. A transformation. A way to make herself
into someone who has no problem belonging.

She tries to put the anxiousness out of her mind.
Reportedly, the entire movie crew has shown up for the
occasion, as though it's something historic. And apparently several hundred people are pushing up against
the Reno police line, trying to catch a glimpse inside
the casino. A press corps worthy of a world event patiently waits, squatting and leaning against poles and
walls, but ready to spring into action at a second's
notice. And she laughs a little, thinking about the
hubbub, knowing it's hardly the Chilean earthquake
or the Greensboro sit-in or Kennedy's nomination or
anything like that. But, she supposes, maybe their being outside does make it *something*, and the idea that
leaving this trailer and stepping out onto the curb in
order to play against Clark Gable might have that level
of importance brings back the anxiousness, and all she
can do is curl herself up tighter, and lift her face into
the airstream, and let it continuously refresh.

Nobody can remember if Harrah's Club has ever been
closed to the public—it's always open, twenty-four

hours a day, 365 days per year. But John Huston has a commitment from the casino for three days, figuring it might take that long to get the shot. And now it's a shell populated by a Hollywood crew, seventy-five extras brought in to act as patrons, and the regular Harrah's staff, still earning their hourly wages, were supposed to go about their business behind the tables and in the pits while trying not to show their disappointment at having to forgo their usual tips. Standing near the entrance, Bill Harrah tells people how he hopes the shoot will go a little quicker; the closure could cost him close to $50,000 per day. The deal was that in exchange for the casino, Huston will ensure that Harrah's is mentioned by name in the film. At one to two days, the potential PR payoff made it seem like a smart financial move. Three days will take it into an area of risk.

The room teems with life, looking oddly normal with people milling about, despite the absence of the usual soundtrack of slot machines and tumbling dice and spinning wheels. As a precaution, the crew elected to cut the air conditioning, thus avoiding potential sound issues. Not even noon, and the inside temperature has become unbearable.

She moves across the floor, her entourage in tow, heading toward the bar, where the scene will be shot. She's acutely aware of the attention she's garnering from the extras and the staff. But it seems misplaced. Her camaraderie is with the crowd. She shares the same anticipation. Darting her eyes around the room with as much expectation as the fans, she also hopes to catch a glimpse of Clark Gable.

Despite the authenticity of the casino, they could be shooting anywhere. The dominant architecture of the bar is the usual ubiquitous construction of spots and floods, and clipboards and notebooks, and cameras and dollies, and electrical wires and film canisters, all supervised by a crew that seems too numerous to fit in such a tiny space. Kneeling beside the large Mitchell camera, Huston peers into the viewfinder that sticks out from the side, waving the stand-ins into place and calling out, "Stop there . . . No, no, back up. There . . . Now, just a little bit more." Evelyn Moriarty inches back and forth on set under his commands, wearing the exact same costume that Marilyn will be wearing in the scene, a long-sleeved black dress with a matching lace-netted hat trimmed in black. She looks like a foggy reflection. Huston slowly backs away from the camera, cautious not to lose his perspective, and confirms with his key grip, Charles Cowie, and his cinematographer, Russell Metty, that they've locked in the lighting values.

Marilyn stands to the side, like an oddly misplaced interloper. She hasn't seen Gable yet. She's fooled for a minute when she sees his stand-in, Alabam' Davis. She folds her arms over her stomach. There's a knot there, both queasy and painful.

Dressed head-to-toe in black, Paula Strasberg steps up to her. Paula came in from New York to ensure that Marilyn stays true to the method she studied at the Actors Studio. She stands a physical contrast to Marilyn, shorter and rounder, with hard features that are shadowed under a strangely oversized bell-shaped hat secured by a strap under her chin. Her expression is serious at all times, and it's made clear to everyone around them that she's there to work for Marilyn, not for the production company. (Marilyn already had to scold Arthur once for giving Paula the sobriquet "Black Bart.") Paula coughs into her fist, then clears her throat. She asks Marilyn if she feels ready. Her voice has an edge. She clips the ends of her sentences, just letting them drop. Marilyn says if ready means knowing her lines, then, yes, she is ready.

Having moved around so much in her life, she's become an acute student, studying everybody around her, watching how they interact and learning how to take and give the proper social cues. On many levels it's served her well: she knows how to fit in, play the various games, and move herself beyond being a social interloper and into someone who is part of the chosen circle. But she's able to hold on to that for only so long. Out of nowhere, an anger will creep up on her, one that's stoked with resentment over having to be the one to adapt, and having to adapt to a convention that sooner or later reveals its true mediocrity. To negotiate the chosen world, she has to conform to the chosen world. And that's usually the point when she'll give in and fall apart. When she's conformed so much that it swallows her whole.

She leans over and whispers to Paula, "I'm going to leave."

"Leave?"

"Yes, leave. I'm going to go."

"They'll ask questions. Someone will want to know why."

"I'll collapse if I have to stand here any longer."

"I can't tell them that, my dear."

"It was just a statement of fact, not an excuse."

"Although, you are looking pale. Still, that's not something I'd say."

"They'd be waiting for that. Expecting it. For me to be sick."

"Yes," Paula says, "they'd be expecting it. Waiting for that."

"I don't want to be standing here when he arrives. I don't want to be just standing, waiting my turn, while everybody fawns, and there is all the drama. I just don't want to be standing here then. It won't be good for the scene. It'll be awkward, is what it will be. Maybe my trailer. There's nothing odd about going back to the trailer, is there?"

Paula takes her by the elbow. "If we work on your lines there, then there's nothing odd about going back to the trailer. It's always helpful to keep on the lines. That's what's good for the scene."

"You know I know them, the lines. Maybe just a little more practice on how to live in them. How to react, you know? And then when he's here, actually ready to go, then we'll come back. Meet him when we're ready to begin. Instead of this standing around. And waiting."

Paula leads her out through the casino, past the rows of inactive slots and card tables guarded by peering extras. Marilyn trails a slight pace behind her, like a shadow. She looks back once to the set. Evelyn waits, opposite Alabam' Davis, hip jutted out and her eyes turned downward, kicking her heels against the floor in boredom. And Evelyn suddenly looks like a child, miscast and out of place, with no business being there. Marilyn turns and pulls even with Paula, wanting to tell her to hurry up or she really will collapse, except that she can't speak because she's holding in her breath. It's what keeps her upright and weighted down. Just enough to get her to the privacy of her trailer, where she can safely collapse from nerves.

Gable tells Marilyn it's good to meet her, and he looks forward to making a good picture together. He says it's a heck of a script that her husband put together, and that sometimes you don't need to say a whole lot to say everything. And she just stands before him, unsure of what to do with her hands. She feels little, as small as she was when she'd lie on her stomach on the bed thumbing through magazines just to find a picture of him. She calls him Mr. Gable, and he corrects her, saying to call him Clark, and she calls him Clark, but it feels as unrealistically dreamy as sitting in any one of her childhood rooms, staring up at the ceiling and imagining that her unknown father might have been Clark Gable. Or that one day Clark Gable would rescue her. *Clark.* He looks at her when she says his name, waiting. But she can't think of anything to follow it up with, and the hole just hangs there, while she searches for something to fill it, until she finally grabs Paula's hand and says, "Have you met Paula Strasberg? My acting coach." As soon as she says *acting coach* a sense of rank amateurishness washes over her, and she follows up by explaining that Paula is married to Lee Strasberg of the Actors Studio in New York, where she's been studying, but Gable just looks at her with no real expression, clearly not interested in where she's been *studying.* In her head she tells herself to shut up, because that's what she needs to do—she needs to shut up. Paula steps forward to introduce herself, and Gable tells her it's good to meet her (no different from how he said it to Marilyn), adding that she must be awfully hot all in black. Marilyn's sure he takes none of this seriously, and so she searches and searches for some bit of information, some interaction she's witnessed that will tell her what to do and that will establish her as something more than a grade-school girl who raised the most money in the school auction, with the prize being a chance to meet Clark Gable. "If you'll excuse me," she says with abrupt alacrity, "I think I left something back in my trailer." She turns around, walking off without Paula, figuring that by the time she reaches her dressing room, she'll be alone and able to rummage through every stored box in her memory, tossing out the contents without anybody else there to name them, until finally finding the one deportment that will allow her to ease into the world of *Clark*, and belong there.

Here's the scene: The four principal characters are staged at the bar. A recently divorced Roslyn has just walked through the casino with Isabelle, who stops to throw a coin in a slot machine. Settling at a table in the lounge, they order a scotch and a rye-and-water. Isabelle tries to cheer Roslyn, telling her, "One thing about this town, it's always full of interesting strangers." Gay Langland, sitting at the bar beside Guido, will first come into view when he turns around to look for his brown and white hound, Tom Dooley. A fairly simple and static scene. Easy enough to stage.

But the dog will not cooperate. Perhaps it's the energy surrounding the set. Or the large crowds outside. Or the electrical buzzing from the cables snaking around the club. Either way, his handler, Cindy James, can't get him under control. She's a veteran trainer, and, as with the rest of the crew, she's been brought on to *The Misfits* because she's the best. She studied under the great animal handler Frank Inn at Halsey Canyon in Santa Clarita, moving from acolyte to torchbearer. But Tom Dooley doesn't care about her professional credentials. He jumps on the barstools, tries to lick

Marilyn's face, wants to engage Gable in some kind of play, and sometimes just runs circles around the bar and through the equipment. As she crouches beside the camera, James's hand signals are blatantly ignored. Tom Dooley will not let them set the scene. It's all Cindy James can do to calm the excitable hound down enough to get through rehearsals. She looks exasperated, trying not to apologize, but rather to explain that he'll come around, he's been trained to perform under any circumstances, he just needs to find his grounding.

Gable looks bothered. He glances from the bar to Marilyn while she strokes the dog, armed with a bag of treats, a quick concession to appeal to Tom Dooley's innate sense of purpose. Catching her eye, Gable holds a longer stare. This is not the way movies were made when he started. If someone couldn't handle the scene, or couldn't even make it on time, then they were fired. And that went from the lead to the dog. She tries to return the look, matching his stern and professional expression— one she recalls Arthur having in a disagreement with a stage director. But her confidence mostly melts inside her. And she worries she might have just lost all her lines.

Once the cameras are rolling, though, Marilyn finds her way into the role, and the lines spill out as if they're not memorized. And though Marilyn Monroe still has little sense of how to get through to Clark Gable, Roslyn Taber and Gay Langland connect on a completely spiritual level, dancing around each other in inaugural questions, accented by her coy looks and his hardened stares. She loves when they shoot the takes. It's barely even acting. She looks up at Gay, her shoulders dropping, with a faint smile on her face, moving treats back and forth to Tom Dooley's mouth. She pulls at her hair. Strokes her neck. Looks right at Gay when she addresses him, but then drops her eyes flirtatiously to finish the lines. She comes alive when Gay justifies living out on a ranch in the countryside, saying how everything is there and in the country "you just live." Her face ignites at that thought, sparking half a blink with her right eye, imagining the possibility, as she says, "I know what you mean." And when she agrees to go and see the ranch with Gay and Guido and Isabelle, surrendering with a devil-may-care laugh, the expression is so real it appears to be something the camera has accidentally caught.

After they wrap for the day, she's backed up into the corner, in conference with Paula about her techniques and delivery. Paula tells her it went well and that she looked beautiful, and she'll be able to offer more once she sees the rushes and can then confer with Lee by phone. There's nothing much more to say. But Marilyn keeps the conversation going. Asking questions. Rehashing. Talking about anything. Anything, until she can see Gable leave, ensuring that she won't find herself trying to figure out how to talk with him.

The next day she almost doesn't show up. Arthur's anxious. Pacing their room at the Mapes Hotel, worrying over some possible changes in the script, particularly the nagging detail of who pays the check in the Harrah's Club scene. There are a few ideas that he needs to talk out with Huston. He's been trying to keep his temperament even while waiting for her, calling through the bathroom door that they need to get going. Reminding her of the schedule. She says to go ahead without her. She'll meet him there.

Arthur knocks once more and this time slowly turns the knob, cracking open the door. She's kneeling before the tub, her white robe still on, the terry belt hanging between her bare legs. A hand is under the faucet stream, testing the temperature. "For God's sake, Marilyn," he says. "It's a ten o'clock call."

She glances back over her shoulder, trying to keep her composure. Her hand slices in and out of the faucet stream. The water's getting too hot. She turns the spigot, inching up the cold water. Hot water droplets rain off the side of her palm, falling into the tub, breaking up near-perfect soap bubbles.

She can hardly look at him. Even her smile has to be oddly forced. Lately, she's had a sense that she's required to subscribe too much to his way of thinking. As though her part of the bargain to be taken more seriously is to appropriate his worldview. And she's been sensing that despite all the platitudes, he doesn't really take her seriously as an artist or as an intellectual. All the acting classes and stacks of Russian literature have been treated more as precious or charming. A project. His Eliza Doolittle. He spends much more time diagnosing and analyzing her than exchanging ideas. Her natural instinct is to reject this relationship as if it were some transplanted organ. She's done it twice before. But she's trying to fight such an urge. Instead, she wants to believe in Arthur. See this film as his gift. A gesture to her. But his manner toward her hasn't seemed to change. His condescension keeps eating away at her. She's feeling more and more without purpose. If her own husband doesn't see her as serious, how can Clark Gable?

Somewhere between a plea and a directive, she tells him, *"Please* just go." And she realizes she's shouted, and although she'd likely have raised her voice anyway, she tells herself it's due to trying to be heard over the running water.

Arthur says he doesn't like this one bit, that it's not the way people do business. But on this morning, she can tell he's more dedicated to getting the script changes set than arguing with his wife through the cracked door of a steaming bathroom. He's going to let it go. Give in. "Just please don't hold us up," he says. "Please."

She walks alone into Harrah's Club two hours late. Her driver, Rudy Kautzky, moved her safely through the spectators, opened the casino's door, and delivered her into the hands of the security team. He then rushed back into the white Cadillac, turned off the flashing red hazard lights, and steered the sedan toward the reserved parking spot. Unlike the previous day, the room is stagnant. The extras lean against the tables. Harrah's workers cluster, conversing in low whispers. The red carpet appears even darker, like spilt wine. Members of her entourage busy themselves with their work, hardly looking at her, both relieved that she's arrived and slightly embarrassed for her. Arthur, slumped in a director's chair, glances over the top of his script, then returns to marking it up, licking the tip of the lead before writing. She strolls back to wardrobe, moving along the perimeter of the bar, conscious of keeping on the opposite side of the room of Gable. He's seated by himself, at one of the tables. His chin cupped in his hand. Staring off at the windows.

She has no regrets and will not be sorry for keeping them waiting. That time was what she'd needed. And other than throwing on her dress and a minimal veneer of makeup, the past two hours were spent in the bath at the Mapes, her arm draped along the side, fingers dragging over the white floor tiles and tracing the lines in the grout. By herself and relaxed. As though in her own private game of house. Periodically she drained the tub, then refilled it with clean water. Watched the soap bubbles rise.

Nobody says anything when she appears costumed and made up, ready to go before the camera, only John Huston announcing the take.

Perfect timing. She can go right into being Roslyn.

Late August 1960: Mapes Hotel, Reno

Monty's on fire. The word is that once that sono-fabitch puts aside his bullshit and gets to acting, it's near impossible to catch him; keep the sauce and junk out of his system, and he might just be the one who surprises you, the one who will very quietly give this movie its backbone. Gable holds steady, the planet everyone circles around; he may be the very reason Monty has been able to keep it together. Gable doesn't talk much; he's fine with letting his history speak for him, happy enough to drive across the desert in his tan Cadillac, film his scenes with a craftsman's ethic, and betray any lack of composure only when it gets too unfocused on the set, or someone tries to settle for *good enough*, or the histrionics go on high. But for the moment, everything is sailing, on a real jag, and it seems as though the bumps were just bumps, and dramas merely reactions, and Huston has the whole crew believing that this is just where the picture's supposed to be, and they're all so goddamn happy, *oohing* and *ahhing* as though watching the finale of a Fourth of July fireworks display, all except for Marilyn, whom nobody seems to be saying anything about, who on set has been either tucked away in her trailer or huddled in consult with Paula Strasberg, trying to get her lines straight. She doesn't know why nobody notices how hard she's working for the role of her life. And she asks that of Arthur, sitting across from him in the restaurant of the Mapes Hotel in Reno, while he cuts at his steak as if the blade were dull or he's using the wrong side, back and forth and back and forth, with nothing to say, and that alone seems impossible: this man who spills words onto the page can't find even one word to say to her. Not even the wrong one. She says, "Why?" and he says, "*Why*?" and she says she doesn't understand *why*. She came into this picture at the top of her game, she tells him. A Golden Globe for *Some Like It Hot*. Intensive training at the Actors Studio. At the top of her game, she says. At the top of her game.

He says, "I think they do respect you."

"Ha," she says, watching him try to cut the meat with the edge of his fork.

"What do you want from them, Marilyn?"

"What do I want?"

"Yes, what do you want?"

A dog trots down the sidewalk, passing by the window. The breed isn't clear. His fur is mussed, sandy with spots of brown. The dog looks to be a mutt but has a poise that suggests breeding and lineage. He appears obedient. As though trained. He wears a thick brown leather collar without tags. No owner in sight.

"There are two different versions: what I actually want," she says, "and what you want me to say."

Arthur gives up the cutting and pushes his plate away. He looks around the room, as though trying to get a waiter's attention. "This is getting ridiculous," he says. "This whole mess. We barely talk, and when we do talk, you bring things up that make us not want to talk again. Only you would try to clean up a mess by making it messier."

She says, "Like I ever clean."

"People have a limited scope, Marilyn. They can look only one place at a time. One direction. They're just not looking in your direction at this very second. Simple."

"Easy for you to say. Because they do respect you." She cuts herself off. "Look," she says, motioning with her forefinger for Arthur to turn around. "He's just waiting." And for a moment they both stare at the dog, now sitting before the window, in elegant posture. Statuesque. She says, "It's like he's there with a purpose."

"I'll stick with version one," he says. "The first one."

Her stare stays fixed on the dog. "I don't follow."

"Version one. What *you* want."

"Yes. What *I* want." She leans forward, leading with her shoulder, her attention still trained on the dog, who hasn't moved. "What I want," she says, "is to know why. Why I can't get even the same breath of respect as Monty or Gable or even you. It's not like . . . You know, the truth is I don't even presume respect anymore. I just want to know why. That's it."

The dog lifts his back leg and scratches behind the ear.

Arthur says, "I once knew someone in Brooklyn who was lying in bed when she heard someone break into her apartment. She hid under the covers and dialed the telephone. But she didn't call the police as you might expect. She called her father. All the way across the country, out on the coast. And you know what her father said? He said, *Why are you calling me? Get off the phone and call the police for Christ's sake.*"

"And did she?"

"That's not really the point. The point of the story."

She sips at her water. The glass fogs around the ice. "You always skip the parts I want to know."

"I guess I wonder who you would have called. That's my point. In a situation like that."

"Let me see . . . Probably someone just to get me through it. Like a shrink."

"Of course you would."

They sit at a corner table. The sun is blocked by a cloud. A shadow starts to fall over Reno. Heat waves still ripple along the pavement. The dog sits, waiting, staring ahead, except for when he startles at the sound of a passing car, but even then he just watches it roll by, turning his head with confidence and dignity before returning his stare forward. His tongue hangs down. Ribs bellow in and out.

She says, "Someone really needs to get that dog some water."

Arthur turns around to check, then looks back at Marilyn. "He's fine," he says. "He belongs to someone, and that someone will take care of him."

"Maybe you can get the waiter's attention. At least he could bring out a bowl of water."

"I'm telling you, he belongs to someone. You can tell by the way he's sitting. Responsibility has not been abdicated."

"That makes him any less thirsty?"

"The thing is," Arthur says, "they do respect you. You just don't see it, is all. You aren't able, I guess." The side of his hand accidentally knocks his water glass. He catches it before it spills. "They respect you because your role is at the center of the movie. All the other characters find their meaning through Roslyn. She is . . . you are the key that allows everything to happen. The fulcrum."

"Does that translate to respect?"

"I'm saying their level of respect has nothing to do with you being Marilyn Monroe. If that's what you're looking for, that's the problem."

"Always the problem."

"You want the whole world to measure you on the various scales of Marilyn Monroe. You just want to be duly noted and commended for jumping from *that* Marilyn Monroe to *this* Marilyn Monroe . . . Applause sign, please."

She rearranges the silverware, exchanging the knife and fork. Straightens the napkin on her lap so that it sits perfectly in the middle. Then she reaches for her purse. "Did you ever order my champagne? I thought I'd asked for one when we sat down." She rarely blinks.

He motions for the waiter, pantomiming pouring a glass of champagne. "I suppose you're right, somebody needs to get that dog some water. The mercury's rising by the second. And whoever owns that dog seems to be taking his sweet time. Especially for an August afternoon."

"I guess responsibility has been abdicated."

He smiles, starts to say something, but then smiles again. It's a way about her. Even at her most maddening she can be charming. The waiter arrives with a bottle of champagne and two flutes. Arthur tells him just one, please. He's not having any today. In part it's vigilance, not to be drawn into a drama. But mostly it's because it's the middle of the afternoon, and there's still rewriting that needs to be done, specifically making the ending work symbolically, figuring out who will cut the stallions loose in the final scenes.

Although the filming of *The Misfits* is back on track, her instincts about wanting respect are not without merit. Because while Monty has been on fire, lately she's been off, and she knows it, and the whole crew knows it; they're handling her with kid gloves. It's almost obvious beyond repair, and the very fact that the crew treads lightly only makes it worse, forcing her to try harder, which works against the very method of acting she's been developing. When she should be in submission to her character, her conscious mind takes over. It's mechanically guiding her as though it's a chapter-by-chapter owner's manual for her body. Arthur and Huston have been telling her she's imagining it. And Paula reminds her to go inside herself. Earlier, they were filming at the rodeo grounds in Dayton. Monty's character, Perce, was poised for a risky bull ride, as Roslyn begged him not to do it. The cameras were rolling. Marilyn took her mark, went down deep for the emotions, as Strasberg had trained her. The lines came out like an overdramatic lead from a high school melodrama. Though she had some awareness of it, she was unable to control it. Initially she figured it was all in her head, that her impression was distorted. But seeing the rush, she realized how out of joint she in fact was. At the same viewing everybody was praising Monty, talking about him as if he'd pulled the nails out of Jesus's hands, talking like she wasn't even in the scene, all except Huston, who told his AD Tom Shaw that maybe he ought to suggest a rehearsal before the retakes tomorrow. In the distance, she watched Monty prep for his next scene, the one in which he was to come up dazed and disoriented after being bucked. He was tossing himself up into the air, then falling smack dab onto the hard pack. Then back up. And again throwing himself into the air. Everybody was in awe. They weren't paying attention to the rushes anymore. Just watching that sonofabitch Monty. On-fucking-fire.

She digs a prescription bottle from out of her satchel. In a single, fluid motion she opens it with just her thumb. "To get me through someone breaking into the apartment," she says. She pops a pill into her mouth, chasing it down with champagne. Swallowing, she looks over Arthur's shoulder, and then to the waiter. "Please get that dog some water," she calls. "He's going to drop otherwise."

With the second sip she empties the glass. Marilyn leans close, drawing Arthur in. She doesn't want to say what she's about to say too loudly. She confesses that while they were filming the scene with Monty yesterday, she forgot his name, his character's name. She says, "I mean I know his name. I knew it. But I just couldn't remember it. Couldn't remember his name was Perce."

"It was a long day. Hot as hell out there."

"No. I don't know how to . . . I knew his name. I know all my lines. All of them. I know everybody's lines. I just can't remember them. It all goes funny, and then blank. A mean streak of white."

"The picture's been rough, is all. A tough shoot."

She pours another glass for herself. Puts the bottle in the middle of the table. It blocks off part of his face. "No. That's too easy. It's got to be something more."

"Such as?"

"That's what I'm asking you."

"Look. There are only about two pages of the script where you don't have a line. There's a lot going on. It's understandable to confuse things. Not to mention, as I just mentioned, that the heat is unforgiving. It's a wonder any of us still know our own names by the end of the day."

She nods. "You don't think I thought all about that?"

"Of course you've thought about that."

"And I don't buy it. You know how you always want to tell me what the *thing* about me is? *The thing about you, Marilyn . . .*"

"I guess this is the part where you tell me the thing about me?"

And she tells him no, that that *thing* belongs to her. She looks him square in the eye, and she wills all her focus on him, careful not to break the eye contact, because she needs all the strength that can possibly be summoned to say what she needs to say. The *thing* about her is him. Look at his script. He's written her to be the version he romanticizes. Her knees tremble. It's no longer his intentions at stake—it's his writing. She wills the pill to dissolve and expand into her veins faster. It's about the script, she says again. She's memorized the lines, held them like something you grip, but she hasn't been able to take them inside. She's afraid she'll never be able to be Roslyn until Arthur allows her not to be *his* re-creation.

"So what are you saying?" he says.

"I don't know how to say it any other way."

She finishes her champagne, letting her stare fall away, as though loosing a giant exhalation. Outside, the waiter crouches down with a bowl of water for the dog. He taps the edge, in order to draw the dog's attention. He just looks at the waiter, cocking his head, and then trots off without sipping, neck slightly bowed. She thinks of how natural gas really has no odor, that the companies add the sulfur smell purely as a warning. For one's own safety.

Arthur pushes his plate away. "Now what?" he asks. "I've got a lot of revising to do. I'll be up all night. Again."

The next morning she complains of fatigue and a general sense of malaise. Phone calls are made back and forth. Between Arthur and Huston. Huston and the producers. The producers and her doctors. By that point she isn't involved. She can't make sense of anything. They discuss her as though she's someone else.

Finally, Marilyn is driven to the airport. In record-breaking temperature, she crosses the tarmac wrapped in a wet sheet and then is flown to Westside Hospital in Los Angeles. Thoughts swirl through her head, none of which are comprehensible, bombarding her like random lines from the script. And she can hear the rest of the crew holding her responsible for further setbacks, and saying how they had figured it would've been Monty who'd screw them up. Such thoughts make her more worn. She just hopes Gable doesn't think any less of her.

That would really get to her. Even before she arrives in LA, her doctor, Hyman Engleberg, indicates she'll likely need to stay at least ten days in order to recuperate. Even from afar he can tell she's that wrecked, both physically and emotionally. Dr. Engleberg insists that he isn't saying whether or not filming needs to be suspended, only that Marilyn likely will not be available during her recovery. She can already hear the producers and crew milling around the Mapes. Already giving up on her, and demanding that Huston send Arthur back to salvage the script so they can continue shooting in her absence.

Once at the hospital, safely dressed in a johnny and a robe, she sees in the mirror how terrible she looks. What has been eating away at the inside now shows itself on her face. It isn't really ugliness, as she's first prone to believe. It's resignation. As if the muscles have given up and the bones have gone flaccid. Everything collapsed.

Mid-September 1960:
The Misfits Set, Pyramid Lake, NV

From a distance it doesn't look that powerful. The nose of the train fans down on the tracks, cutting a straight edge across the desert. It hardly looks as though it's moving at all. An almost perfect curl of smoke rises from the stack, never breaking, maintaining perfect form, keeping pace with the charging locomotive. And as you

ADAM BRAVER

stand by the edge of the track, half looking out across the plains where, in the distance, they're setting up the shoot, you can make out the second-unit guys talking with Huston, who is barely looking up; and the makeup boys sit in the makeup chairs, while Agnes stands over Evelyn, teasing her hair, and the gaffer gauges the light against Evelyn's dress. The sun has barely risen. They've given up on makeup, most of it sweated off as soon as it's applied. So they're just waiting on the shoot. They don't look like much out there, specks in a Nevada desert, but you know the expressions on the faces of every single one of them. As if they're staring you down.

You're on the way. That's what they've been told. The driver has been instructed to tell them you are on the way. That you just wanted a little fresh air. That you are walking the rest of the way in. Walking it off, both the night and the morning. And you know Huston will say, *In the fucking desert?* and maybe some smart-ass will add, *She thinks she's Moses*, and Gable will just shake his head, while Monty closes his eyes, thankful for the extra time, willing a hangover away.

And your husband will stand with his arms crossed, his gaze fixed on his feet. On occasion he'll lick the sweat off his lips and push his glasses back up to the bridge of his nose, holding them in place, believing they won't slip down again. He'll think of the pills, but won't talk of the pills, because he doesn't really understand—despite all that seriousness and intellect, he doesn't understand. *They're needed for sleep? For waking up?* But his biggest fear is that you won't show up. Because he's created *The Misfits* for you. Put his playwriting career on hold, in order that you can be seen as you really are. He's thought up the plot, and the characters' internal struggles, and the way they symbolize the modern world. He knows the way it's supposed to go. He rewrites the lines every day. Throughout the night too. Argues with Huston about his vision being captured just right. He wants to make sure you're taken seriously, just as you want to be, but every day and night seem to be another battle about why you won't be seen as serious or smart. And he makes like he's supportive, but you want to call bullshit on him because you know what he really thinks, because you went up to the hotel room for a forgotten call sheet when he wasn't there, and you saw a bound notebook on the desk by his papers, and you opened it to find it was his diary, and though you knew it was wrong, you still turned the pages, looking at each one with half-squinting eyes like you might look at a car accident, and most of it was boring, mundane steam-blowing about issues of the filming and the script changes, but near the most recent entries you noticed your name, and you read the same passage over and over—the one he wrote about how easily you can embarrass him when you try to engage in anything intellectual. And you wanted to rip the page out and tear it up a hundred different ways, but then you figured that would be just what he'd expect from you (the subject for the follow-up entry), and so you closed the diary, carefully placed it back so it was just the way you found it, and swore to yourself that you would never forget what this felt like. This was more real than any declarations of support.

The ground starts to tremble as the train moves closer, a bit larger though still slight. It smells. The coal cooking. An oil perfume on the wood cross-tracks. And you wish you had a penny to lay down on the rail. Place it with precision, pulling your hand away quickly. You'd watch the coin tremble, dancing for balance, trying to steady itself until the train wheels rolled over it, stretching and elongating Lincoln and changing the penny from something of value into an oddity.

You really should've been on set by now. You've promised that *from this day onward . . .* But you like being a speck in the desert. The location hasn't scared you the way they thought it might. In a strange way it's made you feel more special, as if you stand apart, not by lights or sex or power or money, but by being clearly defined against the barren backdrop. It makes you feel more alive.

Your husband seems to notice you. He says something to Huston, then raises his arms up like a castaway, waving and crossing them to get your attention. Maybe if you stay perfectly still, don't move an arm or break your stare, then he'll think you haven't seen him. He turns to Huston, and Huston knocks his boot into the ground and then spits into the dust cloud he's just made. Your husband's arms still wave, and then he walks toward you, and he seems to be moving faster than the train. You try to keep still, looking past him, so that he's no longer in your sights. If you don't see him, he doesn't see you.

The ground shakes harder. And you hear the groan of the train. It swells inside you, almost making you sick in the stomach. Almost too sick to work.

Late September 1960: *The Misfits* Set, Pyramid Lake, NV

She notices the mustang bleeding, a cut across his chest. He's bound on the desert floor, beside the pickup where he's kept before he's needed for filming. They're prepping the scene in which, after being moved by Roslyn's distress, Monty's character hijacks the truck, drives out to the horse, jumps from the cab, and cuts the stallion free. But the horse already has a gash. And she stares at the thin strip of blood, trying to get a closer look, while Monty's stunt double, Dick Pascoe, tells her not to get too close, that this one is a real fighter. Marilyn, in her white dress shirt and blue dungarees, stamps around the back of the truck, unsure of where to turn. Dust from the dry lake bed follows her. It's as though nobody notices the wound. And she begins to believe she's the only one who cares.

She catches Arthur's eye. "He's injured," she says. "Right there." She points. "Right there."

Arthur squints, looking over at the truck. He's wearing a Western jacket that looks out of place on him. Hanging off his frame, it makes him look boyish, costumed. He keeps a steady composure. One that has become his constant manner when talking with her. And it only enrages her; she sees it as a management technique that seems forced and modulated, as ill-fitting as his Western jacket with its dark suede and cowboy swirls. "The horse is fine, Marilyn," he says. "He just scraped himself a little on the wire over there." He glances at the temporary corral, where thin slats of wood stand to form a mushroom-shaped pen held together by three parallel rows of wires. At least a dozen horses crowd the open end, while the narrower mouth feeds into a large animal trailer. "It's just a scrape," he says. "Nothing more."

"No." She shakes her head. Hands opening and closing into fists. "Can't you see he's injured?"

"Marilyn, I'm telling you the horse is fine. It's what they do. Sometimes animals get hurt. And then they heal. It's what they do."

Behind the truck, a dolly rolls on a sheet of plywood, steadying for the shot. Huston stands beside it, reviewing the sequence with Pascoe, who will rush out with the knife to cut the ropes and set the mustang free. And then he'll shoo it away and run like hell back into the cab. The horse is just too unpredictable to send in Monty. Huston says they need to do it quickly and they need to do it right. This is a one-chance shot.

She goes over to Huston, leaving Arthur behind. She walks in a heavy patter that breaks into a jog. "John," she says. "John. No."

He waves her back, not turning around.

"No, John," she says, but her voice can't seem to rise above a whisper. "Let him go. Cut the scene. Let him go. He's hurt. We can't make him continue. Can we forget this take? For now?"

Huston motions to Pascoe to go. In the single take, Pascoe is able to jump out, dash around the truck, brandish his knife, and cut loose the trussed horse. The mustang squirms and twists upright, then leaps up, making straight for the corral, where it runs a series of quick circles, darting in and out among the other horses, in and out of the horse trailer, and then finally settles down, rubbing up against the temporary planks of the very fence that brought on the injury.

It's hard to read Huston's expression, between the sunglasses and his long-brimmed cap; it's sometimes hard to tell if he has any at all. Marilyn waits, shoulders drooped, her arms hanging, as if they might pull her straight into the ground. She's positioned almost exactly between Huston and Arthur. Huston finally looks at her. His head cocked. "Well?" he says, a yellowed smile rising. "What was it you wanted?"

She knows they're waiting. She's already missed the call.

Sitting on the edge of her bed, she fiddles with the wire hood from a champagne bottle, pushing her index finger in and out of the tiny cage. She's phoned down once to the front desk to say she's ready and to ask if the driver is there yet. They've assured her they'll send him up immediately, once he arrives. She said it's just that he might be out front idling, and the desk clerk repeated that he'd send the driver right up, his manly voice turning boylike in its irritation. She pushes her finger deeper into the opening and twists the wire, tightening it until the tip of her finger turns red, and then a puffy white.

The lip of a champagne bottle pokes out from under the bed, on its side. She rolls her heel over the curved glass, rocking it back and forth.

It's all spiraled so quickly. She can't remember if she told Arthur to get his own room, or if he came to that himself. She can barely remember when the conversation took place. Only that she screamed. But that was that. Again she finds herself huddled in her own room. And while it's always been lousy being by herself, there is a comforting familiarity. She's begun to accept that every step forward is really just a step into the past.

Negative forces exist. They're part of the electricity that turns the world, the essential charge that comes from the polarity of the negative trying to touch the positive. And in the past, the solution has been simple: Just don't show up. A tactic that's always been more than basic avoidance, one that's about survival—not having the internal wherewithal to deal with the crap being thrown at you. It's overwhelming enough trying to battle your own complexities, but to step out the door and be assaulted by everyone else's is a near-impossible task. Especially when you're just trying to stay steady—keep a clear head and an even presence. So it becomes easier not to go (or at least delay going as long as you can). And, yes, it's annoying to the others, she knows that, she's no fool; but what they don't understand is that it's better for everyone in the end, because if she succumbed to pressure and expectation and showed up when she wasn't ready, then her defenses couldn't handle it; her state of mind would be left completely vulnerable. She'd fall apart right then and there. And, yes, maybe she is like a child, unwilling to believe that bad things in the world can't be kept away. But she still can't help but cling to the long-held belief that if she closes her eyes, then those bad things won't exist in the first place.

She looks at the phone and considers calling downstairs again. The car should've been here already. It's Gable she worries about, waiting under the desert sun, how the heat can burden a man his age. He's been looking a little more peaked each day. And, as with her, it's seemed harder and harder for him to maintain the energy; he too comes alive only when the cameras roll. She's never meant to keep him waiting, and she thinks he knows that. He understands how hard it can be. You never mean to bring harm. You're actually trying to keep it away. She reaches for the phone, about to turn the rotary, but the wire hood is still clamped over her finger. She tries to shake it off. And then, pinching the pointed end, she twists it just enough to slide her finger out. But it seems her twisting actually compresses the hood, and before she can stop, a thin line of blood bands under the ring. And she sits there, staring at it, her mouth as dry as can be, unsure of what to do, her foot still on the bottle, watching the blood pool and fall in small drops on the sheet, where it expands and blends like watercolor. Should she loosen or tighten the hood? What would best keep the blood in?

From the Mapes, it's still an hour-long ride out to Pyramid Lake. She pictures the day turning cloudy, with maybe even some rain coming. And everyone waiting for her. But no matter what the sky ends up looking like, the desert will still be unbearably hot. It's impossible to imagine being out there, lousy under that heat. But that's not why she's running late. Nothing's ever as simple as the weather.

Late September 1960: *The Misfits* Set, Pyramid Lake, NV

She channels Lee Strasberg, hearing his instructions over and over (contact those memories of emotion, *remember the emotions*, keep them in storage, *always be emotionally available*). And she stands by herself on the dry bed of Pyramid Lake, facing a semicircled crew that's drawn far back, setting up the long shot of Roslyn screaming against the vast plain, ringed by the snowcapped Sierras. A single boom is set behind her. She wears a denim jacket that matches her Levi's, and she tugs on the collar of her white shirt as she thinks through her lines. She's confused herself about how to play the scene. Caught up in the logic of the sequence, when she knows it's really about the unconscious. *Acting*, she can hear Mr. Strasberg say, *is not something you do. It occurs.* And there she stands, preparing for what very well may be the soul of the picture, seeing Roslyn in the terms of the cultural world she's become part of in New York, but still not sure if she can connect with the emotional world that Strasberg has taught her is so critical.

The choreography requires her to spin and to turn and to fall apart while calling out the men who've captured the horses, telling them they're murderers. Her final monologue is a plea to keep things from falling apart. There will be no close-ups. Just a body trying to keep upright and balanced on a world spinning too fast.

Arthur paces, almost nervously, jabbering at Huston, scribbling notes and changes, then leaning over to show Huston the clipboard. Gable slumps in a director's chair, the one with her name written in script. He pulls his jacket closed; his ten-gallon hat shades his eyes. He'll be dragged around the lake bed shortly—he insists on doing his own stunts—and for the first time in the past three months he looks truly exhausted. Earlier in the day, he announced that his wife, Kay, is expecting. That thought alone must have drained him, maybe even scared him. But he took the handshakes and the hugs with a joyfully honest reception. Since then, he's barely moved from the chair. Just stared down at his feet.

Everyone huddles around the cameras, waiting for instructions. She stays put on her mark, trying to keep her character until Huston calls action. Then Huston slips behind a curtain in the back of a truck, coughing his way in like a sputtering engine. He probably needs to review the second-unit footage to make sure all the values match before they do anything else.

Arthur continues to pace, inching toward Paula. Marilyn has hardly talked with him since they've taken separate rooms. It isn't because she's angry or resentful. She just has nothing to say. He's been keeping his distance. Trying not to incite anything. He looks so prepared for the movie to fall apart. So nervous. Afraid that in these final days she'll fail before the camera. He says something to Paula, and she nods slowly, as she always does, and then gives Marilyn a hand signal, pushing her open palms up and down as a reminder to keep calm. What strange bedfellows: Arthur, who's detested Paula all along, who thinks of the Strasbergs as cultish, now seeks camaraderie with her. Is he that worried? Has he not noticed that the *least* likely place she'll fall apart is before the camera?

Wind rises. Shadows creep along with the dust. But she keeps moving. Dancing in place. Shaking her arms out. Rolling her neck. Mouthing her lines over and over. Just holding out for the clapboard. A rag doll waiting to come to life.

Huston pushes back out through the black curtain and climbs down off the flatbed. He claps his hands, and stamps his boot, and, as though it's a staged illusion, momentarily disappears amid a cloud of alkali dust. The crew gathers around him. He swats away the dirt. Turns his head to cough behind his back. Paula motions for Marilyn to come in. Shooting is suspended, Huston declares. He explains that full daylight is needed to match the scenes, and the overcast sky and late-afternoon shadows make that impossible. They'll resume tomorrow. Marilyn senses some people looking at her, as if the weather too is her fault.

Gable jumps up and dusts off his jeans. "Well, then," he says. "I'll gladly be taking the afternoon off." He's going to go look at Bill Harrah's car collection, he says. It's the one thing in Reno he actually wants to do. Someone asks if arrangements should be made for Kay to go along—have her picked up at the Mapes. Gable shakes his head, saying the only old things she likes are actors. Others follow with their own plans, laughing about how the whole picture is so over budget that it hardly makes a difference.

Marilyn isn't paying attention. She watches the sky, willing the clouds to move, to blow on by. But they stretch as far as she can see. Covering the blue. Hiding the mountain peaks. She doesn't want Huston to strike the set. She's fixed to shoot the scene. It isn't about knowing her lines, or about being prepared with her blocking. It's about that unexpected moment when the character completely overwhelms you, and is ready to come out. Sometimes it just strikes. Like that. And she would use all her remaining breath to blow away the clouds if she could, saving just enough life to release before the camera.

Forgetting the people around her, Marilyn walks back out across the lake bed, almost wandering, and ends up returning to the spot for Roslyn's soliloquy. The desert light turns yellow, almost opaque, with the smell of a sky about to change, a fragrance somewhere between sweet and stale. The boom has been collapsed and taken down. The horse trailers are driving away. The spots are already in their crates. Gable has left, followed by much of the crew. Alone, she forces herself to inventory the exact emotion of what it feels like to be Roslyn in this moment, but she tells herself not to think about it, and hates herself when she does.

Mid-October 1960: *The Misfits Set*, Pyramid Lake, NV

The camera pulls in tight on Gable. He's laid out on the ground, dressed in leather chaps and boots, his gloved hands holding on to a rope tied to a truck, preparing for a stunt that will simulate him being pulled by a wild horse. His hair is mussed, and his face, sweaty and chapped from the wind, looks both worn and rugged. Makeup will be applied to further the appearance of wear, but salty dust from the lake has stuck to his face as though expertly detailed. It takes strength just to lie there and wait. Huston leans over him, moving the tripod a little more to the left, framing the shot, and then saying to pull the camera in tighter.

The exterior scenes have been shot. It's how time was utilized when Marilyn showed up late, or when they weren't sure if she'd show up at all. The second unit filmed horses running wild across the plains. Even though Gable declared he was doing all his own stunts, his stunt double, Jim Palen, still came in for the rougher long-distance scenes involving the horses. Even Gable knew that was too dangerous. It was further emphasized when Palen was kicked in the side of the head by a wild stallion named Boots during the second-unit takes in which the horse is supposed to simulate kicking a fallen Gay. A hoof landed right near the temple. When Palen just lay there, some thought he was dead, or at least brain-damaged, until he finally muttered a few words and sat up. But he was lucky, if it can be called luck. And no one could really call it an accident, because they were wild horses, and that's what wild horses do. It's been noticed, but never said, that danger seems to come only when Marilyn throws off the schedule. It's occurred to her, too. The idea that coincidence might be the true link between apparent cause and effect scares her, and rarely does it exhilarate.

Gable is to be dragged by the truck across the lake bed, about four hundred feet, while the camera hangs back for the long shot. Then they'll take it again, shooting in tight from another camera mounted on the side of the flatbed. Gable agrees that the truck should drive at a regular speed, about thirty-five miles per hour, the pace of a horse, so that his body will twist and bump the way it should, because for all the time it's been taking to make this picture, already twenty-five days over schedule, they might as well get it right. They'll have plenty of time, he says. It ought to be at least a couple of hours more before Marilyn makes it out there. After all, the call is only two hours old.

With a parched voice, Gable says, "Can we get this thing going, already?"

Huston, squinting through the Mitchell's lens, mumbles it will be a few more minutes.

"A few more minutes," Gable says. "A few more minutes." In order to rest his neck, he puts his head down, then lifts it back up quickly, spitting off a layer of dirt stuck to his lips. "This whole film's been a *few more minutes*."

Marilyn arrives as he's being dragged for the second time. The flatbed is driving in a straight line, with a cameraman tilted over the side, and Gable just barely hanging on to the end of the rope, snaking in all directions. He's on his side, and his body bounces and twists, and for a moment it seems it could be a stuffed dummy (not even a stuntman!), because the body bounces so freely, rising up with a floating lightness, and then thudding down violently, in a way no one should have to endure. And it pains her to see Gable as just a body, one that's easily beaten and easily bruised, no different from the next. There was a dog who once lived next door to one of her foster homes, and one day a neighbor came out holding a hoe, and he told the barking dog to keep quiet, and when the dog kept at it, the man lifted up his hoe and he sliced the dog in half. That's how it is when people are after something for themselves. There are no concerns about consequences. They'll rip you to shreds. Just to keep their world in order.

The news from Vegas is good today. Bookmakers there have posted Kennedy as a 6 to 5 favorite over Nixon in next month's election. The shift is major, as Nixon had been running 8 to 6 just last week, perhaps up-staging the report in the papers that George Gallup believes neither he nor anyone else can "predict the outcome of the November presidential election with scientific accuracy," a reminder that the real forecast-ing always falls to the oddsmakers. And maybe this news brings a sense of hope, especially given a recent report, called "Community of Fear," released by the Center for the Study of Democratic Institutions, that anticipates that as the arms race grows, the United States will be forced to move underground, to build factories inside caves, along with apartment build-ings and stores. Meanwhile, the *New York Times* has posted a headline that warns "Caution Is Advised With Dark Lipstick," and the article goes on to say that "when wearing a blackened red lipstick, do not wear brightly colored eye make-up. The new black eye-shadow looks best or a dark blue shade. Do not wear rouge." This evening she's going with Arthur to a party Huston is throwing at the Christmas Tree Restaurant in honor of Arthur's and Monty's birthdays, and she's conscious of wearing a darker eye shadow, not because of how it looks but because it feels a little less dangerous, which she understands is not the same as safe. And she will accompany Arthur because it's his birthday, and they are still married, and those things still matter, even if it means she'll sit sideways, scrunching herself against the town car's window, watching the pines cascade down the side of the Mt. Rose Highway, not saying a word the entire ride up the twisting hill, sick with an unidentified nervousness that she figures will only be cured by a shaker of gin and one of the loose Nembutals at the bottom of her purse, cure enough until she can get back to her own bed, and back in front of the camera the following day.

When they arrive, the Christmas Tree Restaurant is jammed. Their whole Hollywood herd has filled the dark lodge. Even Huston's mother is there. One day away from wrapping the final scenes, and everyone in the company is falling on top of each other like it's premiere night. Some sit at the dinner tables carving into their steaks, faces tiger-striped by candlelight. Others crowd around the fireplace, offering toasts and playful salutations. Most spill into the bar or gather around the game tables. But where's Gable? He's the one person she doesn't see.

Standing at the craps table sipping a martini, she peers around the room, trying to catch sight of him. He doesn't seem to be anywhere. Finally, she asks Huston if he's seen him. And Huston says Gable begged off. His body was too sore from all the thumping. All those long days in the sun and the hot winds have just about taken it out of him. So he stayed in for the night. Battered and worn.

Marilyn doesn't say anything. And though she doesn't suspect she's been accused, she feels accused.

She throws back the last of her martini and then scoops up a pair of dice off the table. She shakes them in her hand. Huston tells her to throw them. "Come on, honey." But she keeps rattling them. Almost able to hear them turning in her palm. Changing in combination. Each die catches the scab on her index finger cut from the wire hood. Slow, stilted tumbles, before turning over to the next number. Make it a lucky one. She tries to remember the percentages. Calculate the odds. And she swears her palm is filling with blood. Flooding with it. "Don't think," Huston says, stamping his boot. "Just do it."

November 1960: Los Angeles

By November, Gable is dead. He was at Hollywood Presbyterian Hospital for ten days, following a heart attack late on a Saturday night, a day after he shot his last scene on Stage 2 at the Paramount studios, where, at least for him, *The Misfits* had wrapped. He was in his house when the pains hit, the whole chest cavity constricting and tightening, and it felt like one minute longer and it would strangle him and crush his ribs, while Kay, no stranger to heart issues, recognized the symptoms at once and phoned for the ambulance. Over the course of the ten days he seemed to be progressing, getting cautiously positive reports from Dr. Cerini. Kay, who was six months pregnant, was set up in the empty room beside his. She sat with her husband at all possible times, trying to keep his hand on her rounded belly, and while he slept she had her own heart condition monitored. Hollywood visitors came with occasional news about the editing of the film, although nobody really intended to bother him with that kind of talk; it was more to let him know that the life he was part of was going on normally around him (while for some of the industry people it was really all they knew how to talk about). But on the morning of November 17, his heart rebelled again, and when it was done he lay with his head thrashed into a pillow, eyes open, not in peace or in fear, but in somewhat furious defiance of his hospital bed, while the nurse shouted for Kay, and the doctors didn't bother with pretending. His last day had been his best. Alert and looking far better than his true condition. On that day, Gable stopped thinking about his heart and instead talked to his wife about their unborn child, apologizing to Kay for putting her through this while expecting, and swearing he'd get better, be a father and husband who could stand for his family, and maybe it was the fact that he stopped thinking about his heart that gave it the chance to give out. This man who'd spent a lifetime and career believing only in vigilance. Who'd allowed himself to be dragged around the Nevada desert, waving away the stuntmen, because he couldn't give a face to Gay's anguish unless he felt the physical bumping and the physical bruising. Otherwise, he would just be acting.

In Projection Room 5 at Paramount, Huston works furiously with his main editors, George Tomasini and Doc Erickson. They focus as though they're starving, watching take after take, debating points of view, second shots, lighting, cuts, angles; reel by reel, they work to put this movie together with a little more urgency. With Gable's death, the studio wants to push up the release of *The Misfits*, get it into the theaters sooner. Huston doesn't fight it. He justifies the studio's decision to capitalize on the situation by rationalizing that if he can beat the December 31 screening deadline for the Academy Awards, he should be able to get Gable a nod for the nomination. Gable's work is that good, he says; he deserves an honest shot at next year's Oscar. And so they trim and they shape and they splice and they stitch to bring the multitude of pieces to life.

In the middle of his hospital stay, on Armistice Day, Gable received a telegram from President Eisenhower encouraging him to stay strong. Eisenhower had had some experience in these matters. He wrote not to worry. Stay strong. To do what the doctor ordered. And not to get angry.

On the same day, across the country, at one thirty in the afternoon, under the awning at 444 East Fifty-Seventh Street, where Marilyn had returned to live, her assistant, Pat Newcomb, announced to a hastily gathered group of reporters that Marilyn was separating from Arthur Miller. Although it was emphasized that there were no plans for a divorce at this point, Newcomb did make clear that the parting was amicable, the result of several meetings between Mr. Miller and Miss Monroe (she pointed up behind her to Marilyn's apartment), all arranged and negotiated without lawyers. Miller didn't say anything publicly but is reported to have told people close to him that there was no chance of reconciliation. Marilyn didn't come down during the announcement. Never weighed in. Newcomb said she wasn't yet dressed.

Gable is buried at the Forest Lawn Memorial Park in Glendale, California. Nearly five hundred people crowd the Church of the Recessional, with another three hundred gathered outside. The *New York Times* describes the coffin as being "blanketed by red roses, atop which rested a small crown of miniature, darker red roses." Because he was a major in the air force, he's given a full military funeral—an air force honor guard stands over his casket, while Johnson West, an air force chaplain, delivers the eulogy. And Hollywood, of course, is present—sprinkled throughout the pews, and most notably among the pallbearers, whose ranks include Spencer Tracy, Jimmy Stewart, and Robert Taylor. Gable's remains will be entombed the following week, taking their place beside his third wife, Carol Lombard. An empty tomb waits on the other side, for Kay, when the time comes.

Some time later, Kay Gable is quoted as saying it was *The Misfits* that contributed to her husband's heart attack, specifically "the eternal waiting" on the set. The quote is interpreted by some as an implication of blame directed at Marilyn; her inability to stay on schedule throughout the filming, either showing up late or not coming in at all, and the emotional stress that would've caused Gable, not to mention the physical stress of having to wait around in the desert heat. Kay Gable denies any intention of indicting Marilyn, and, in fact, she later invites Marilyn to the christening of the newly born John Gable. But still it eats away at Marilyn. That she may have been culpable in the death of Gable, whom she idolized and relied upon for as long as she can remember, is too much for her.

It's one thing to wave the gun in your own face. It's another thing when it accidentally fires in the wrong direction.

July 27, 1962

Cal Neva Lodge, Crystal Bay, NV

Talking to a reporter for the Las Vegas Review-Journal, *Phyllis McGuire, of the singing group the McGuire Sisters, reflected on how Sinatra "never could understand" the stigma of friendship with Giancana. She had the insight, due to the McGuire Sisters regularly playing the Celebrity Showroom and, more importantly, due to her being Giancana's girlfriend. McGuire said, "He'd been friends with the boys for years." In filing his report on October 11, 1962, the special agent of the Chicago field office (name redacted) made sure to note that "GIANCANA SHOULD BE CONSIDERED ARMED AND DANGEROUS SINCE HE HAS A VICIOUS TEMPERAMENT, A PSYCHOPATHIC PERSONALITY AND IS KNOWN TO HAVE CARRIED FIREARMS."*

On October 6, 1959, Giancana appeared for fifteen minutes before a federal grand jury in Chicago to testify in an investigation of "hoodlum control" in the Rush Street belt, a downtown nightclub district. The Chicago Sun-Times *reported that "Giancana growled obscenities at the United States Court House and broke into seemingly meaningless prattle 'tomorrow is tomorrow is tomorrow is tomorrow.'"*

6:25 PM

———

    * Elizabeth Arden "Pat-a-Crème" makeup
    * Erno Laszlo blush, face powder, and cream
    * Helena Rubinstein mascara

These are among the items in her zippered carrying case. Many primitive cultures dress in masks and costumes to frighten off their enemies.

Standing in front of the bathroom mirror, she draws on lipstick, then traces the edges with a darker lip liner. Behind her, the lake is a dark splotch beneath a passing cloud; it has swallowed up any trace of sunlight. The two large pines directly in view are only shapes. Within the hour, she'll make her way to Frank's show. It seems like that will be the best place to actually disappear. Somewhere on a song.

She thinks about this character, Marilyn Monroe: someone who has been under constant fire but has always assumed herself safe.

Or, it's as if you're trying to do something as simple as light a cigarette, but you end up burning down the house. And everybody's screaming, hollering, and the place is a stinking nightmare, but all you can do is stand there with a butt dangling off your lip, thinking, "I wonder if I can catch a light off one of the flames."

That's more what she's like.

The wrinkles in her evening dress need smoothing. She palms down the fabric over her hips; the darted seams show off the dress's construction. Then she cranes her arm down in one smooth gesture toward the bed and scoops up a scarf out of the valise. She nearly loses her balance, trying to stand straight again.

She folds the scarf into a triangle and wraps it around her head, tying it loosely under her chin. It could be the weather. Or the dyes. Or maybe something has changed hormonally. But she's lost control of her hair. It resists a brush. Collapses under the sprays. It's just best covered up. Held down and hidden. No one needs to know what's going on under there.

7:40 PM

Pat Lawford is elegance; she wears a sleeveless black taffeta cocktail dress, conservative, with only a slight, almost futuristic, slit cut into the top, not really meant to reveal her cleavage, but instead to display the double strand of pearls strung around her throat. Her hair, dyed dark black, is pulled back and combed tightly against her scalp, enunciating the Kennedy familial jawline.

A cocktail waitress pushes through the crowded casino floor, overfilled drinks sloshing on her tray. The lodge's dark red carpets contrast perfectly with the pinewood walls and the buckhorn chandelier dangling over the center of the game room. A real rustic getaway. The waitress turns sideways, passing right behind Pat and Marilyn, who have just found each other, the ridge of her rear scraping Marilyn's hip.

Maybe it's the scarf over her head that's kept her unnoticed, but she's passed through the room nearly invisible.

Pat turns to Marilyn, looking her straight in the eye. As though they're the only ones in this crowded area. "Now back to what I was going to tell you on the plane."

"Oh no," Marilyn says. "I remember that I said I wouldn't forget. But you know what?"

"What?"

"I've forgotten what I wasn't going to forget."

In a burst of sentences, Pat delivers her news. On the airplane, she says, it still had been speculation, something she'd heard through her assistant just before the car came to pick her up. That's why she'd been keeping it from Peter. But now it's confirmed. She had her assistant check in with a contact at the hotel. Pat hesitates, as though pausing for effect. Her eyes widen. Sam Giancana is here. Somewhere at the Cal Neva. As soon as Sinatra's plane dropped them off, it turned right around and headed back to Los Angeles, where it picked the mobster up and delivered him to Reno. She nods three times, holding her mouth tight. And then continues, saying he was chauffeured to the lodge in the very same car that had brought them here earlier. How sick is that?

Marilyn listens enough to be companionable, but her attention is on the room; she watches women drop coins into the slot machines, while men dressed in dark, shiny suits, with pressed shirts and skinny ties, smelling of Pall Malls or Viceroys mixed with spicy colognes, crowd the gaming tables. It's not that she's immune to Pat's worries; it's more about vigilance. She understands how easily she can be infected by these dramas.

Pat says she's going to insist that Frank fly her out first thing tomorrow morning, and she'll even tell him why, no matter what Peter might think. She can't be expected to be in the same place as a well-known gangster who has somewhat publicly declared war on her brothers for targeting him in their campaign against organized crime. It's insulting. Not to mention a little bit threatening, the way Giancana rants about her entire family, always spitting out their surname as if it's some kind of rot. What was Frank thinking, if he was even thinking at all?

Although she doesn't say anything, Marilyn is surprised Frank would allow Giancana to stroll around the lodge. It's not so much about Giancana, she's had some good times with him, but it's fairly common knowledge that Nevada keeps a Black Book of known gangsters, and that any casino that serves one will lose its license. But, she reminds herself, that's not her problem. None of this is. She just can't let herself get involved.

"Maybe you can just ignore him?" Marilyn suggests to Pat. "Keep away from him."

"Just keeping your distance," Pat says, "doesn't make something go away."

She swears she sees Joe at one of the craps tables. His hair is grayed slightly along the temples, and he looks appropriately distracted and disgusted, standing tall among the rest, still carrying an athlete's stature. Would he have defied Frank's dictum just for a closer watch over her? She looks again. But he's turned his back to her.

Stepping in time with each other, she and Pat move tentatively across the floor, toward the red padded doors that lead into the show room. Pat says she wants to find Peter before Frank's show starts, before he gets caught up in all the hubbub of being in the inner circle. She's going to demand that he take this seriously. She wants to tell him they're leaving in the morning. All three of them. She says that Frank will take notice when he sees Marilyn leaving; then he'll understand the magnitude of the line he's crossed.

Marilyn lifts a glass of champagne off the tray of another passing waitress, nearly upsetting the balance of the tray. She sips as they walk, part of the champagne spilling down her chin, then dripping onto the front of her dress. Like a child, she wipes her mouth with her forearm. Little brown-blond hairs glisten under the lights.

By the lounge entrance, in the short hallway between the show room and the restaurant, Peter Lawford stands, hands in his pockets. He appears to be waiting for someone; his darting eyes suggest someone trying to assume a tactician's pose. He understands the principles of being observed. Locating himself in a place where he can see and be seen. It is crucial for him to stand apart from the crowd. To clearly be on the inside. Muffled music seeps out from under the door. Buddy Greco, first on the bill, sings about searching around the world, his lyrics moving over a quick walking bass line. A pair of women comes out of the Joseph Magnin, a modest storefront satellite of the elite San Francisco department store, shopping bags in hand, nearly bumping into people making their way to the show room. Peter's fumbling for something in his pockets, and when his hands emerge, he's pinching a book of matches. He plucks a Tareyton from his palm and dangles the cigarette off his lip while striking a match. In the past, Pat has confessed to Marilyn how much it bothers her that Peter is obsessed with keeping pace with Sinatra and the rest of the so-called Rat Pack. And because he's never quite achieved the stature of the others (particularly Frank, Dean, and Sammy), he's somehow stayed at their whim, aware of being only the occasional member (or as Frank calls him, the brother-in-Lawford). Because of that he jumps. Answers invitations and suggestions and directives with a desperate haste. His marrying into the Kennedys only further complicated things. And while he has been part of building the bridge that's conflated politics with show business, his instincts always tilt him toward glamour, and for that, Pat has said, his judgments have more than once put everybody in awkward situations.

It's strange how clearly Marilyn sees this scene. As though getting a glimpse of what it means to live on the outside.

Peter taps his ashes onto the red carpet, steps over them, avoiding one little orange ember, and kisses his wife on the lips. Marilyn, still sipping from the same glass of champagne, looks toward the show-room door. Peter stares at her, double-taking to make sure it's her underneath the scarf.

Pat starts in about needing to go back to LA in the morning. Peter holds his cigarette between his thumb and index finger away from his side, listening, vaguely amused, as though it's not the first time he's heard this kind of talk. Looking at Marilyn instead of his wife, he starts to justify staying, delivering a quasi lecture on rumor and innuendo, mistaking Marilyn's willful indifference for disappointment at the prospect of having to go back to LA. Leaving would be rude. He says even if it were true that Giancana was somewhere in the hotel (of which, he repeats, there is no proof), the insult to Frank would outweigh the insult Giancana's presence would bring to Peter's in-laws. They all need to realize they're bigger than potential threats.

Marilyn tries to look away from their disagreement, thinking about how she can leave.

A woman slips out of the Celebrity Showroom, loosing a rapid-fire snare drum down the hall.

Turning from her husband in irritation, Pat mouths to Marilyn, "This is unbelievable." She stops. Tilts her neck and squints. "Don't you think so?"

Marilyn nods, and her scarf comes undone, the ends dangling over her ears. She pulls it off, down over her face, and then balls it up in her hand. Her other hand reflexively touches her hair, patting it into place. Her lips are tight. Sucked back against her teeth. Drawing in close to Pat, Marilyn whispers with a certain force, "Don't look, but everyone is staring at me as if I just suddenly appeared."

9:45 PM

People begin taking their seats. The show-room spot-light cuts in and out, its dusty stream focused on the microphone stand just to the right of center stage. Violinists hunch over, facing each other. They drag their bows across the strings, listening to one another, carefully sharpening the flats. Guitars ping between the E and the B strings, getting in tune, back and forth and back and forth. Near the piano, a sleeve of sheet music slips from a stagehand's fingers to the floor. He bends down to pick it up, then places the loose page on a music stand, silently apologizing through a stilted smile. Meanwhile, a snare drum is being tightened, the numbing repetition of the smacking hardly noticed.

These are the cues.

Anticipation shapes the crowd.

Just to the right of the main doors, she sits in Sinatra's booth, waiting for him to take the stage. There are some places where you instinctively feel comforted, and for her the show room is one of them, with its contemporary art hanging on opposite walls, telling the history of theater through a series of pieces in wire and fabric and paint, a cross between the primitive and the abstract. In the curved red velveteen box, not much different from the others lining the back of the lounge, she's scooted all the way in, near the center, at the apex of the curve, with a direct sight line to the stage. Pat

Lawford sits to her right, blocking the entrance, keeping watch over the room. In the box is a small table, a thin layer of wood supported by two heavy metal stands. On the tabletop, rows of champagne bottles and martini glasses and flutes and tumblers make for something of a glass wall, or maybe tools strewn around a work site. Half-smoked cigarettes still burn in the ashtrays.

Frank was just there, anchoring the left side of the box and greeting streams of well-wishers, until he realized he had to leave to get ready to go on. Peter began to follow. Pat whispered to him that he'd better keep away from Giancana if he's back there. She looked so serious. Marilyn sipped her champagne, looking down but still listening, despite all her best efforts. Don't tell him anything about anything, Pat instructed her husband. Nothing about anything.

There is another, more private booth upstairs beside the lighting crew, almost impossible to see from the floor. And then there are the backstage tables, easily accessible from the tunnels, nearly impervious to surveillance, for those who need to be impervious to surveillance. Marilyn rejected Pat's suggestion that they sit in one of the more secreted spots, as though it might be safer. She likes being on the show-room floor, where she can feel the kick drum thumping against her chest, and the horn section breezing over her face, and then Frank's voice melting all that away and taking her with it.

She picks up a water glass. She's parched, and there's hardly enough for a sip. Even the ice is gone. She looks around for a waiter. The closest one is all the way down the aisle, near the tables in front of the stage, leaning before an oddly mismatched couple, engaged in a conversation that already has gone on too long. She keeps half an eye on the waiter, watching him straighten up and smile at what should be the last comment from the woman. He keeps turning his body, shifting his stance, trying to break from the banter.

Finally free, the waiter walks up the aisle. When it looks as though he might notice her, the lights go down, and the crowd claps enthusiastically.

She tries holding her glass up. But it just disappears, right beneath the emerging spotlight.

In his tuxedo and bow tie, Frank hits the stage. He enters stage right, smiling and bowing to the wings before moving to his spot just left of center. He slips the microphone from the stand, right in time with the band launching into "Get Me to the Church on Time." He takes small steps, skirting along with the beat, his snapping fingers motoring him like an outboard engine. She loves his carefree side, which was missing earlier in the cabin. He repositions the mic into the stand, raises his arms with palms exposed. His chest and lungs open, preparing for a long note. And when he does reach that note and then belts it loose, he seems momentarily to hold the song between his palms, guiding it to the left and then back to the middle before finally releasing it.

Pat leans over, her head is bobbing. She says, "He's really on tonight."

Marilyn nods. "Don't you just love it?" she says. "You can always count on him. He gives you a bang that snaps you right out of wherever you've been." She reaches across the table for one of the other water glasses, partially full. But Pat pushes it away. "No, Marilyn," she says. "Who knows who's been drinking from that."

"What's that?"

"I said, who knows who's been drinking from that . . . Here, wet yourself with some champagne."

Up front, a woman turns and glances at their booth, squinting through the lowly lit show room. Her discovery is cataloged in whispers and elbow nudges, causing the whole table to look. Marilyn waves at them, throwing along a little smile. There's that secret split-second recognition, when she can see the surprise of the unexpected, and then almost feel it like the electrical jolt that can jump-start a heart.

Frank pauses for a brief aside when he forgets the words, but even that seems smoothly perfected, as though, if not part of the act, it's an element of charm essential to his personality. And now the band is soaring, and sometimes it seems to bump him in the hips, as though it will lift him off his feet, but then his arms come down right on the beat with the horns and the snare drum, and it's clear he would never be swept away; he is the anchor. His eyes are glassy, but his focus is intact, and at the end when he sings *ding dong ding dong*, there's whimsy in his eye, and again it seems personal and private, as though for this one time only he's willing to let you in on it, to share in and be part of his world.

He loves the swing. She can almost see him swooning between Jupiter and Mars in "Fly Me to the Moon." It's knowing but honest. And in that moment she's in his otherly sway, swinging between those planets with him. Never planning to return.

Marilyn says, "When he's on the stage, Frank can make you fall in love a hundred times over."

"In one set."

"One set? I'd say in one song."

After a few numbers he stops the band. He wants to say hello officially. "Not only in song," he says, "but to chat with you for a minute." He thanks everybody for being there. He tells them they're marvelous and reminds them that without an audience, "We're dead. D-E-A-D."

Is he looking right at her?

"Now," he says, "where's the bar?"

And then (again she swears he's looking right at her) he launches into "Please Be Kind."

The waiter has come with another bottle of champagne. He used to say, *Courtesy of the chairman*, but now, after he's worked the cork from the neck with his back half turned to the stage for the millionth time tonight, he just leaves it. The bubbles sizzle in the glass, and she sways side to side, and she remembers why she accepted the invitation to Tahoe in the first place. Nights like these infuse a sense of life right into your bloodstream. They push the lawsuits and all the jazz that intends to beat up on you right off to the side, where it sits exposed for what it's worth—a load of crap left behind by those with half the talent and half the ambition who want to prove that they are in control, and that they control the likes of you. It's a surgical procedure, being in this room right now. The music is lifting their dead weight right out of her, like those psychic surgeons in the Philippines she's read about in the news. She can feel herself going with it. And what more can she do but raise her glass and drink a toast to that?

Pat looks over at her. She too is smiling, but her body looks stiff. Her eyes keep glancing to each side of the stage. Her ongoing paranoia could easily break the moment. Finally she leans in to Marilyn, and whisper-shouts into her ear, "Don't lose your vigilance."

Marilyn reaches for her water glass, then realizes she forgot to ask for a refill. "Ha," she says. "Me, vigilant?" And she pours a glass of champagne instead, hoping to derail the conversation.

In closing with "My Kind of Town," Frank pauses to thank the orchestra. After the applause, he places the mic back into the stand, moves it slightly to the side, commenting on needing to be a muscleman with these things, then salutes the audience, again saying that without them he's nothing. As the clapping fades, he points to the doors leading out to the casino. "As long as we're here," he says, "why don't we all have a drink?" He glances backstage with a smirk for a split second, before looking back again at the audience. As the scrim drops, Frank exits to the right, his arms opened wide.

When the lights come up, she turns to see Pat squirming, looking to the sides of the stage in concern, and the crowd is rising and she feels like she's in the spotlight, and she realizes that her going away has all been temporary, it was only as good as Frank's act. And she can feel herself start to wilt, and she's parched, and she reaches for water but the glass is still empty, and she's afraid that Pat will say one more thing about Giancana, and she can't take one more thing that will remotely suggest the world of Marilyn Monroe. She's that fragile.

People stream up the aisles, and they're almost all looking at her. She slouches a little, hiding behind the wall of bottles and barware.

Pat looks at Marilyn, and she says, "Well?"

"I think I'm just going to go back to my cabin." Her mouth is still gummy.

"Without even a nightcap?"

"Vigilance," Marilyn says. "Frank will understand."

A Count Basie recording pumps through the speakers, its rhythms controlling the hurried pace of the floor; the chatter rises and falls in tandem with the horn section. She moves quickly between rows of green felt tables, en route to the tunnel. Pushing around people who step in front of her to get to the slots. Turning sideways, she squeezes through the crowd at the roulette wheel.

Passing in front of the craps table where she swore she'd seen Joe, she slows down for a quick look, checking to see if he might still be there.

Through the yellowed smoke pall, Sam Giancana catches her eye. She'd know him anywhere: heavyset, gray suit, receding hairline. He winks; his black hornrims magnify his eyeballs. He's charming in a raw kind of way. Like a magnificent accident that draws all the attention. But he's always reeked of cruelty, even when he's thrown on the charm. It stinks from the sweat in the creases of his forehead, pooling and glistening, to the breath leaking out the permanent snarl at the corners of his lips.

He waves her over, his hand turning rapidly.

She's unable to break his stare. Forcing a polite smile, she shrugs and keeps moving, holding the backs of occupied chairs at the blackjack tables for balance.

His voice stabs out in a burst across the table, "You can't come over and just say hello?"

She shakes her head, mouthing the word *sorry*, and continues to walk.

He stands, now motioning with both hands. "You already forget you know me, or something?" he says. "For just a moment. Don't be such a stuck-up. Now, come over and bring me a little luck."

Her foot catches under the leg of an empty slot machine stool, halting her in place.

"Ain't that a pip!" she hears, floating slow motion against the pace of the room. "Ain't that a pip!"

Across the room a noise rises, and she glances that way, and she sees a crowd of people pushing through the casino toward the bar, and leading the pack is Frank, and he walks like the grand marshal with a champagne glass as a baton, and she bows her head slowly, because she doesn't want to be noticed, and that stool keeps blocking her way, and she tries to kick it to the side but instead flips it over, startling the people around it, who fan backward, and she doesn't know where to go, only that she has to go somewhere other than here, and fast, and there's Giancana's threatening bellow that she better not just walk away, and from the other side of the floor a poof of laughter from Sinatra's gaggle, and she resists the urge to look, because she can't look: she can't become involved. And it's all at a standstill. Like a frequency that's been jammed.

January–June 1962

January 1962: Henry Weinstein's House, Hollywood

"Yes," she says. She keeps saying *yes*, agreeing with ideas she doesn't quite understand. It isn't that she's afraid to admit her ignorance to him; she just doesn't want him to stop talking or, at least, to change course on her account. "Yes," she says, nodding with a firm expression. "Yes. Yes. Yes."

She's coiled up delicately on the carpet, with her feet tucked under her thighs, a rapt and well-mannered schoolgirl. He sits on the couch, slightly out of place, adding a rustic edge to the finely polished Beverly Hills veneer. His feet, covered by old black boots, the leather scuffed and aged, heels nearly touching, rest by her side. Toes pointing in contradictory directions. Among this Hollywood gathering at Henry Weinstein's residence, he might be mistaken for a character actor, or a displaced avuncular sort. But with Marilyn Monroe at his feet, holding his hand as they talk, her hair dyed to an albino white that matches his, there's no doubt that the great poet, the eighty-four-year-old Carl Sandburg, is the wonder of the party.

She stays by his side for most of the evening. There's something she needs from him. It presses. She's not quite sure what it is yet. Or how to find it. And so she keeps trying at different topics and subjects, telling him about the books she's reading, the ideas they bring up, and though none is quite right, it doesn't make a difference because no matter what he says, and no matter what she can't thoroughly understand, he is talking to her, and looking in her eyes, as though *he* understands, as though they're the only two people in the room. The only two people left on earth.

She sips the last of her champagne. When she places the empty flute on the carpet, it falls over, weightless. One last drop trails toward the lip but doesn't spill out. She asks a server for another, then smiles up at Mr. Sandburg, saying it's best to get a little alcohol in her system now, as she finds trying to get to sleep from scratch just impossible. (Even though he's said to call him Carl, as with Clark Gable, it's hard to think of him in any way other than Mr. Sandburg.)

He says, "Well, gosh, I hope I'm not keeping you up past your bedtime. I always forget about manners."

She laughs. "No. No," she says. "A girl just needs to prepare herself, is all. That's all I'm saying."

"I once read about something called *sleep debt*. A wonderful term, don't you think? Both lyrical and literal." His voice has the melodious cadence of his western North Carolina home, but still preserved around the corners is the harder midwestern clip that blunts the ends of occasional words. "Some say it's modern times that keep us building up the debt of unused sleep. Maybe cutting out a stage or two of the sleep cycle. The *non-rapid-eye movement*." He says it as if it were a new political party.

"I *am* the modern girl. Or so they say."

"That you are. But even the modern girl needs exercise. The best remedy for sleepless nights. Other than, perhaps, a steady, reliable companion."

"Please don't make me talk about that. I was just feeling good."

"A good exercise routine will take you through the sleep phases. And a tired body makes for a sounder rest. Buy out your sleep debt with a little exercise, my darling. That's the key."

One of the servers, an older man of stern expression, hands her a fresh glass of champagne. He glances at the spent flute on its side; she tells him not to worry about it. To save his back from bending, she'll wash the glass later. But he insists on taking it, leaning over to get the flute. She lifts her new glass up toward Mr. Sandburg. "To exercise," she says. "And to a good night's sleep."

Sandburg asks her to put the champagne down for a minute. He rises from the couch. Lifts her by the elbows. They stand inches from each other. The green in his eyes might swallow her. He says, "One can't do what one doesn't know how to do."

At a glance, they seem an oddly familiar sight. He's dressed all in black, with a tie so dark and flat against his chest that it's barely distinguishable. In the way that some aging women begin to take on the hardened faces of old men, his features, conversely, have taken on a feminine softness. Although still in good shape, his body has filled out, shoulders pushed up past the neck, his torso and legs grown more solid. It's as though a certain gravitas has mutated the physical form, drawing him closer to the ground. Meanwhile, Marilyn is ever aware that her body is changing. She no longer has a sassy innocence and youthful hubris. This is not the same woman who pushed snuggly against DiMaggio in New York doorways, blushing in the novelty of her newly created world. Nor is she Miller's apprentice intellectual weaving among the East Coast literati. Her dress, which now falls just below the knee, is conservatively colored tan, with a subversive gabardine weave that makes her shine when it catches the light. It connotes a sophistication achieved only with a certain maturity, yet it still manages to reveal a body holding on to its youth. She came into the party wearing dark glasses, but midway through she replaced them with a dark scarf over her head, like a babushka. A necessity to be partially covered, as though having all her head exposed leaves her vulnerable. Maybe it's the weariness in her eyes. Or how easily her body turns limp when she sits down. But the similarity between Sandburg and Marilyn is not in their appearance, or difference of appearance. It's in the way they look at each other. As though they exist in a world that's familiar only to them. Where the weight of age is not a factor, where the body and the mind do not battle for dominance, and where confessions are not secrets.

Standing with her in the corner of the room, he takes her hands, then drops them. "Now I want you to follow me," he says. "Just do as I do."

She smiles at him. Anticipating.

"You need to take in a deep breath," he says. His voice weakens with the inhalation. "And then put your arms out while you gently squat."

"Gently squat," she repeats.

"With your arms out."

"With my arms out."

The guests at the party stop to watch. Sandburg and Marilyn don't notice. She follows his lead. Out of sync. Up and down. Down and up. Like alternating pistons. "Feel your legs stretch," he says, as he rises.

She crouches; her hemline creeps halfway up her thighs. "Oh, it burns," she says. "But in the good way." She stretches her arms out, trying to keep her balance.

"You're pushing the blood all through you. Reminding your body of the life it has, and its need for rest and replenishment. That knowledge alone should be enough for your body to know it has to go to sleep. You just need to remind it to listen."

She laughs. "I don't know about that. A stiff drink does just fine."

A group of party guests encircles them, smiling, as though cheering someone on in the last stage of a superhuman feat. One woman joins in, trying to time her squats between Sandburg's and Marilyn's. Mr. Weinstein, in the corner, puts on a bossa nova record. Some clap their hands, sloshing gin and ice over the lips of their tumblers. More guests join the exercise routine, dropping up and down with the beat.

As Mr. Sandburg rises, Marilyn drapes her arms over his shoulders. Other than hearing the rhythm of the song, she's unaware of what's going on around her. And while she's tempted to collapse into him, instead she leads him in a dance toward the center of the living room.

From afar Sandburg appears to move with grace, an effortless sway of the hips, guided by the smooth lead of the shoulders. His steps look light, almost skating. But in fact his moves are unsure and awkward. His body struggles for a center balance, and he doesn't really move into the dance as much as he falls into it. Yet he looks completely at ease. Seeing himself as Astaire, Nijinsky, and Chaplin rolled into one. The illusion is only possible because of Marilyn. In her arms he gets to appropriate her grace. And with each beat, each movement, he begins to understand living a life of the body, beyond just nourishing it. Existing almost entirely free from the calculus of intellect.

"You could lull me to sleep," she says, resting her head on his shoulder.

"The last role for an old man."

"No," she whispers, then lifts her head. "No. You misunderstand me."

People dance around them. Some whirl in circles alone, cocktails in hand. Others face each other.

Mr. Sandburg asks, "I don't understand?" and she says, "No. You don't understand."

He rests one hand on her shoulder. The other on her hip. "In that case," he says, "perhaps you can help me understand."

"I don't mean to be insulting."

"That could only be if I heard it that way."

"It's just rare to be at peace with someone at peace with himself. That's all I'm saying. And when you feel that peace . . . Well, you know what I'm saying."

"That it just lulls you."

"But I'm always so tired . . . *Tired*. Not sleepy. I just want a good night's sleep, so I can wake up and start all over again."

He follows her around in a box step, pulling her in. She fits against his body. Almost as though she might've come from it. And she tells him she can't picture it. That all her life she's been able to close her eyes and see herself at another point in the future. She's been able to imagine everything that has come to be. But she can't see herself growing old. She just draws a blank. And isn't that where wisdom comes from? It's just that for the first time in her life she can't picture the future. Or picture how to make it. As Sandburg pauses, thinking before he talks, Weinstein dances up to them, his feet moving in place, and asks Sandburg and Marilyn, "May I?"

Sandburg backs away, saying he assumes Weinstein isn't asking for his hand. Then he nods to her it's okay and mouths, "Just keep dancing." He falls back onto the couch. Reaches for Marilyn's half-filled glass and sips it down in one gulp. He's tired, and his legs are sore, and he's slightly winded. And as he watches Marilyn dancing across the living room in the arms of Mr. Weinstein, a smile on her face as though the cameras have started rolling, Sandburg is envious of her youth. But also slightly saddened. What he has always valued, what has always allowed him to look in the mirror and see himself without the wear that shows in photographs, is the idea that there's still something to imagine. Even though, if pressed, he could never quite tell you what he hopes for, or expects to find, still, it's the possibility that there's something to slow down for, to reach for. And now, looking at her as she shimmies in performance for Mr. Weinstein, it's as though she's become that chicken in the slaughterhouse whose body still runs at full speed long after it's been decapitated.

Marilyn dances away from Weinstein and slumps down next to Sandburg. She drops her head on the couch back, rolling it onto his shoulder. With one arm lifted, she stretches her hand out, waiting for a glass of champagne to materialize. "You'd think that by now I'd be tuckered toward sleep," she says. "Especially after our routine."

"Let me suggest one thing," Sandburg says, staring up at the ceiling.

"Just one?"

He doesn't reply. He closes his eyes. "Let me suggest you build a ladder."

"A ladder." She speaks dreamily, her head sinking a little heavier against him. But her skin buzzes. Electricity skims off her.

"With a lot of rungs. Enough that you can't ever imagine not being able to climb."

"But a long way to fall." She makes herself laugh.

"Well, there's always that possibility."

The champagne finally appears in her hand. She lifts it for yet another toast. "Tell me more things I don't know," she says. "Tell me all the things I should know. The things I'll need to know. Will you?"

"Yes," he says. "Yes, yes."

May 1962: Twentieth Century-Fox Studio
Back Lot, Los Angeles

You arrive on the set of *Something's Got to Give* ready to shoot the swimming pool scene. In an attempt to win back her husband from his new wife, your character, Ellen Arden, will dive into a courtyard swimming pool at night. When Nick looks out from the balcony, she'll call up, "Come on in, the water's so refreshing, after you've done . . . Oh, you know!" Nick, in a panic, will implore her to hurry out of the pool before his new wife catches wind of what's going on. Ellen will gladly oblige, lifting her naked body out of the water and onto the ledge.

At the shoot you slip into a body stocking. Skin-tight and flesh-colored. You were never asked. It was just assumed that a bodysuit made the most sense for a woman your age. You pull at it. Pat your hands against your legs. Over your stomach. Hesitating. Finally, you tell your director, George Cukor, to clear the set, pare it down to the essential crew. He looks at you, unsure. "What," you say, "you don't think Marilyn Monroe would *ever* shoot a nude scene in a body stocking, do you? Really."

"Marilyn." His voice turns somewhat shaky. He clears his throat, trying to regain his composure.

"Now please clear the area. This is between me and the camera."

You strip down to a pair of flesh-colored panties. At the sight of your body, the breath leaks out of the room. Since the gallbladder surgery last year, your figure has slimmed and almost reshaped into one that is stronger and more sculpted. You slide into the pool, weightless. Gliding before the camera, you feel the water wash over your skin. Running up and over your legs, down your back, and collaring your neck. You swish back and forth. Swimming from one end of the pool to the other. And when you speak your lines, you find your voice is a contradiction of confidence and vulnerability. And you want to keep talking because you're intrigued by it. After the take, one of the crew stands over the pool holding out an oversized white towel embossed with the studio logo. You shake your head. Staying in the water, you shimmy out of your underwear, tossing them up to the poolside, where they land with a wet thud. Backing up to the wall, you brace your hands and push up and out of the pool. While you sit on the ledge, your feet scooping at the water, your head turned, looking over your shoulder, photographers snap pictures. As they shoot, you palm your hands along your thighs, feeling your own skin as though it's something entirely new, with a sensuality that belongs to someone else. Every few inches you touch a spot that feels tired and familiar, but you move your hands away quickly. You're about to turn thirty-six. And your body can feel new. Different. Like one that doesn't belong to Marilyn Monroe anymore.

June 1, 1962: Twentieth Century-Fox Studio Back Lot, Los Angeles

The cast and crew plan the surprise party for three o'clock, giving themselves time to throw it together between takes. Marilyn surprises everyone by arriving at the soundstage for the 9:30 AM call, prompt and alert. No one's expected her to show up on time on her birthday. Cukor sees his opportunity to get through the day's scene and possibly get *Something's Got to Give* back on track (or at least keep it from getting any further behind). He declares that before anyone goes home they'll complete the day's planned shooting schedule. The party is rescheduled for six o'clock.

Overseas, the ongoing, bloated production of *Cleopatra* has been bleeding Twentieth. Already ten times over budget, and nowhere near being completed, the filming is now being relocated from London to Rome. And that means new everything, practically starting from scratch. A real debacle that threatens bankruptcy for the studio. Getting Marilyn Monroe out of that New York attitude and back into a romantic comedy (especially casting her against Dean Martin) seemed like the perfect solution for a quick infusion of cash into Twentieth's crumbling accounts. Pressure for a fast turnaround of *Something's Got to Give* has been coming down on the producer, Henry Weinstein, who, in turn, channels it down to Cukor. But, as with *The Misfits*,

Marilyn Monroe has put the whole production behind schedule. Never there. Sometimes sick. Sometimes exhausted. Sometimes both. And when she does come in, her face is heavy-eyed and bloated. Sometimes she can barely talk above a whisper. You wouldn't even know she's Marilyn Monroe.

Cukor rides her hard. He just about hit the roof when she jetted out to New York two weeks ago to wish Kennedy a happy birthday and then called in sick to the set. Now he threatens. Hopes a little intimidation will put her on track before the studio cuts her off. A little dose of reality. And while most of the threats are empty, the jabs about her age do seem to get to her. He drills at her about pushing forty in Hollywood. Says she's lucky to still be cast as a lead, with younger beauties like Elizabeth Taylor out there. She could be playing mothers in barely credited supporting roles. She's getting leads only because her past reputation still carries weight with the box office; but reputations are an easily changing currency in Hollywood. Keep up this shit and there isn't a producer out there who will touch her.

Throughout the day, nobody says a word about Marilyn's birthday. Maybe it's to avoid spoiling the surprise party, or maybe it's because they remember that for some people birthdays aren't always a happy thing to remember.

Four things the stand-in should know:

1. If someone's needed to run up to the farmers market for the cake, say you'll go. Just
   because you are a near-exact match to the
   principal (in terms of size, shape, and facial
   structure), you are not the star. You are not
   her peer. Not her friend. You are her stand-in.

2. To get from the back lot at Twentieth Century-
   Fox to the farmers market, head down Pico
   for about two miles and then take a left on
   La Cienega for another mile and a half, when
   you'll turn onto West Third. You'll find the
   market up the road about a mile, right at the
   corner of Fairfax. By public transportation it
   could take as much as half an hour. By car, if
   the traffic is light, there's no reason you can't
   be there in ten to fifteen minutes.

3. Walk all the way down through the center
   stalls, then bear right just before reaching the
   back. Buy the sheet cake there, at Humphrey
   Bakery. It really is the best option for a birthday party that will be celebrated in the work-
   place. Make sure it can serve at least a dozen
   or so people. And don't get tempted to change
   the order. It's easy to second-guess the order
   when you see the layer cakes and their fanciful

decorations. The sheet cake really is best for the occasion. Seven dollars ought to cover it. Stick with the sheet cake.

4. At the Humphrey Bakery counter, you're not to assume any connection to the star, even though people might confuse you with her because of your hair, wardrobe, and dark sunglasses. You should just approach the counter with polite discretion and say softly, "I called ahead from the studio. For the sheet cake."

On the way to her dressing room, Marilyn passes her stand-in, Evelyn Moriarty, heading to the set, dressed in a replica costume of what Marilyn will soon be wearing for the rest of the day—a bronze suit, fur-lined along the collar, the cuffs, and the hem. Evelyn stops and kicks out her hip: "So what do you think of the suit?"

"That we look beautiful today."

Crewmembers move by, clipboards pressed against their chests, in conversation. They nod at Marilyn but don't acknowledge Evelyn. She tugs on the material at her hip, working it between her thumb and forefinger. Marilyn sneers at their backs on Evelyn's behalf.

Seeing the suit on Evelyn makes Marilyn think she should borrow it for the evening. She mentions that to Evelyn, asking what she thinks, explaining it would be for a muscular dystrophy charity event taking place at Dodger Stadium. Even though the fund-raiser is at a baseball park before a game, it seems like a serious event, one for which she should dress maturely. Joe will be escorting her. With Arthur gone, and now that she's back in California, he's been trying to reassume what he believes is his rightful place. She lets him have it, when it suits her; those times when she just needs to be around someone who believes she deserves better.

Evelyn says, "I'm sure you'd be stunning in it."

"But *should* I wear it tonight? What do you think?"

"I don't think you'll look like a phony, if that's what you mean." Evelyn glances up at the clock. "But I do think I'd better get out to the set. There's going to be a fit from Cukor if we get behind schedule today. And it'll probably come right at me, as long as I'm the one in this suit."

"Perhaps we'll talk later? Catch up."

"If the shoot ever finishes."

"Evelyn?"

"Yes?"

"Maybe you want to leave the costume on? And then you can just go tonight as me?"

By the end of the day, once Cukor determines he has the perfect take, Marilyn changes into her capris and her black-and-white leopard-print shirt. Walking back out to the set, she feigns surprise at the birthday celebration (although she is surprised to see Henry Weinstein). The sheet cake is at the center of the table, with flashing sparklers running down the center. A birthday card is displayed behind it, hastily drawn on a 14x16 sheet by one of the studio artists. It depicts a caricature of her, turned to the side, wearing only high heels and a towel, glancing out with a look of caught surprise, wide-eyed, with a lipsticked mouth open in a baby-faced O. At the top of the page, in a bold red cartoon script, it reads, *Happy Birthday (Suit)*. The cast and crew have signed it along the margins.

Evelyn leads the crew in "Happy Birthday" and then cuts the sheet cake into even squares. People stand while eating their pieces, never really settling. Once Weinstein leaves, the rest quickly follow suit, apologizing for needing to get home for dinner. Soon, it's just her and Evelyn. Each stands at an opposite end of the cake. Marilyn chases a pill down with a Dixie cup of water. She looks at Evelyn and shrugs. "Doctor's orders," she says.

Evelyn begins cleaning. "I'm afraid I have to go myself," she says. "It's an early call tomorrow. But I know you'll be lovely tonight at the stadium. Beautiful on your birthday." She walks around the table, stacking up the dirty paper plates, smashing down the unfinished slices of cake.

Marilyn props up a sparkler, one that wasn't lit. "It's not too late, you know," she says.

"Too late?"

"For you to go. Tonight."

"You make me laugh."

"Really. No one will know the difference."

"You know that isn't so," Evelyn says, dropping the

pile of dirty plates into the garbage can. "You tell Joe I said hello. And I'll see you tomorrow." On her way out, she gathers up the spent plastic forks and throws them out as well, and one more time says, "You know that isn't so."

Marilyn lights the sparkler, its sparks reflecting in her eyes. "I don't know," she says to herself, lifting her arm to wave good-bye, but not looking back. In the shimmering glitter, she begins to see herself refracted, as though looking at another person altogether.

Four things Marilyn knows:

1. In February of 1962, Elizabeth Taylor was thrown a gigantic birthday bash on the set of *Cleopatra* in Rome.

2. Six thousand dollars' worth of decoration and pomp was showered on her, mostly footed by her husband, Eddie Fisher, who was desperately trying to keep his wife from fully falling for Richard Burton. He even gave her a $10,000 diamond ring and an emerald-studded mirror.

3. Reportedly, it was a party worthy of the Egyptian queen she was portraying.

4. Elizabeth Taylor had turned thirty. Marilyn Monroe thirty-six. Decades apart, in Hollywood years.

June 1, 1962: Dodger Stadium, Los Angeles

Marilyn doesn't want to be alone with the woman in the wheelchair to the left of the microphone. They've gathered in the infield, between the pitcher's mound and home plate. Behind them, a multiracial boys' choir in dark sweaters with gold crests is neatly lined up and kicking in place; a coterie of officials and notables take their places, along with the other special guest, LA Angels outfielder Albie Pearson. Joe's there also, but trying to keep a low profile, drawn more to the visiting Yankees than to the festivities surrounding the pregame appeal to raise funds for muscular dystrophy.

Wearing a white cardigan and a checkered shirt, the wheelchair woman sits where the organizers parked her. An attendant waits behind the chair, reflexively caressing the grooved rubber grips, ready to move her at a moment's notice. When the woman stares straight ahead, toward the backstop, she looks poised and confident, dark hair pushed up above the brow, her lips smartly made up and bright. But when she turns her head she reveals her rag-doll limbs. Her whole body appears to collapse, and her facial features turn malleable, forming expressions based on the position of her neck. She keeps trying to look at Marilyn, tilting her head back in a way that will keep a smile.

Marilyn notices this from the corner of her eye and turns her attention elsewhere quickly. It scares her that much. Makes her feel a little queasy. But it isn't about the physical disability or the disfigured form. It's the reminder that even at his most benevolent there still are clear limits to God's compassion.

Despite the cool and damp Friday evening, 51,000 people fill the stadium, greatly anticipating the Yankees' first visit of the season. Mickey Mantle's injury has lessened the enthusiasm somewhat. However, he will be suited up and sitting in the dugout—a worthy consolation. At least that's how Joe put it on the car ride over. *A worthy consolation*. Since they've arrived, Joe has been working the field, making his way from player to player. More than ten years past retirement, and it still lights him up. But it isn't the notice he gets from the fans for being on the diamond that compels him to attend events held in baseball stadiums. It's the familiarity and sense of belonging that come from feeling the way the infield grass gives under his feet. She once asked him what he meant by that, but he couldn't explain it in a better way.

The stadium lights shine down, leaving a slight halo of moisture above Chavez Ravine. Being away from the *Something's Got to Give* set allows Marilyn to move through that glow with a relaxed grace. Her suit, accented by a silver star-shaped brooch pinned just over her left breast, no longer feels like something from wardrobe, but instead like an outfit designed to showcase the best of her. The fur-lined hat sits in perfect complement to her platinum hair, fashionable and unexpectedly practical, keeping her warm on this moist and unusually chilly evening. She even passed

Wally Cox, with whom she had just spent the whole day on set, and gave him a warm, surprised smile, as if she hadn't seen him in ages.

Meanwhile, the wheelchair woman keeps looking. She's trying to say something to Marilyn. Working hard to catch her eye. Make her mouth work while she has the chance. Marilyn, alone for the moment, smiles and takes a step back, looking for a distraction. As if on cue, Joe walks by in conversation with a Yankees player. She reaches out and grabs Joe's sleeve, stops him, and turns him around until he blocks off the wheelchair. "Well, here she is," Joe says, turning around in place. "She's right here."

"Yes," she says, shifting slightly to the side. "Yes. Here I am."

She's introduced to Johnny Sain. He joined the Yankees during Joe's final year, at the end of the 1951 season, when they beat the Giants in six to take the World Series. "He put in a heck of an effort on that final run," Joe explains.

"Barely," Sain says, speaking in a slow Southern drawl. "Couldn't close out the ninth in game six. Three straight hits, and I almost lost it."

"But he got us there, and then some, in the following years. And now he's our pitching coach. Made everybody forget he'd ever been a Brave, much less a National Leaguer."

"Well, I don't know about that." Sain looks over his shoulder to the dugout, and then down to the bullpen, where the pitchers are stretching. "But it's a pleasure to meet you, Miss Monroe. A real honor." She leans in to hear him over the stadium noise. "A real pleasure," he repeats, louder. "To meet you."

From the corner of her eye she catches the attendant backing up the wheelchair, as if it might be changing position for a better view of her. "Yes," she says, straining her voice. "Likewise."

"Johnny says to expect a good one from Terry tonight. That his arm is all gold. He's going to take it to Belinsky and those Angels."

She sidesteps to the right, trying to keep the wheelchair out of her sight line. "I'll certainly be rooting for him," she says. "Rooting Belinsky on."

"No," Joe says. "*Terry*. Bo Belinsky's on the Angels." He winks at Sain with a crooked grin. "We root for Ralph Terry."

"Ralph Terry it is, then. I'll be rooting *him* on."

"Miss Monroe, I will tell him you said that. Knowing that ought to give him a little extra gas."

"Yes," she says. "You tell him."

Sain heads down to the bullpen, with Joe falling behind him. The woman again sits in plain view. And for once Marilyn wishes Joe would stick around, tell her more about baseball or why the Angels played at Dodger Stadium or other things that don't really matter.

She's placed beside Albie Pearson, waiting to be announced. The boys' choir forms a break wall behind them, and the wheelchair is positioned in front of them, just ahead of Pearson. The woman cranes her neck, still trying to catch Marilyn's eye. Sooner or later, Marilyn knows, she'll have to say something to her.

When she's announced, Marilyn looks up into the seats behind home plate. Each level blurs into the next. The crowd cheers, and for just a moment she has to remember this event isn't about her. But after all the threats from the studio, and their insinuations about the demise of her career, it's hard to let the moment go. She extends her arms and claps toward the woman. The crowd rises to its feet. She walks up to the microphone, briskly passing the wheelchair as though she could catch something, and makes her appeal for the charity fund.

The boys' choir breaks into "Happy Birthday"; the imperfection of their nervous voices, high and sweet and lightly off-key, is too real for her. Like a million-watt bulb exposing every hidden frailty and weakening her. When they finish, she hugs two boys in the front row, almost collapsing into them.

Someone takes her hand. She turns around and sees it's the woman in the wheelchair. Summoning what strength she has, the woman reels Marilyn in. The woman's mouth forms slowly, lips finding shapes. Her raspy voice is barely audible above the stadium cheers. Carefully enunciating, she says, "I've only wanted to say *happy birthday*."

On the way home, Marilyn sits with her back to Joe, staring out the window and pinching the bridge of her nose. The cool, damp Chavez Ravine wind got to her. It rattled her sinuses. They didn't stay for the game, which leaves Joe a little quiet on the ride. She told him he should stay, but he escorted her out with the resentment of duty. And it never seemed to occur to him that she actually wanted him to stay. Sometimes she doesn't know what's harder to bear: inviting Joe into her life, or turning him away.

Traffic slows on the Pasadena Freeway, near downtown. The city lights stab at her, bringing on a wave of nausea. Closing her eyes, she squeezes harder on her sinuses. She asks the driver to turn up the radio. She doesn't want to hear her thoughts. They only swell her head. Joe reaches over to rub her neck. His hand is too big. Awkward, without tenderness. She scoots closer to the door, shrugging him away with her shoulders. She doesn't want to be touched.

She wakes the next morning barely able to breathe. The thermometer reads 100. Her face feels like a pressure cooker, the swelling brought on by a relapse of sinusitis. There's no way she can get to the studio. It hurts to move. She stares at the phone. Unwilling even to dial it. When she worked at the Radioplane Company all those years back, she was always afraid to call in sick, fearful of losing her income. There were days when she was so under the weather she hardly was able to see or to think, and yet she still had to stand at the assembly line constructing drones. Measuring the balsa. Cutting. Gluing and assembling. Never again, she would say to herself all the way through her shift. Then she'd say it again driving out of the old Metropolitan Airport, through the farmlands of Van Nuys. Never again.

Drawing in a breath, she phones Henry Weinstein. (The idea of explaining to Cukor makes her feel even sicker.) When he hears her voice, Weinstein's reply sounds wary with anticipation. She starts off with an apology, and then tells him about the charity event, and then the sinusitis that she just can't shake. The bottom line, she says, is that she can't make today's shoot. The fever has thrown her a real knockout punch. It's bad. So bad that when she hangs up she's going to have her maid call Dr. Greenson.

Weinstein is silent.

"Henry," she asks, "did you hear me?"

"No," he says.

"You can't hear me?"

"No. Please."

"I'm so sorry, Henry. I don't want to stop, you know that . . . But this is for real. I don't want this. For real."

"No. No. No."

They both understand this will only lead to trouble for her and the picture. What more can she do but apologize again?

But he isn't even listening. "No. No. No," he repeats.

"I'm going to go now, Henry. I'm just going to rest up good, and get ready to shoot again soon. For a day or so. Whatever the doctor says. But please don't worry, Henry. I'll be back as soon as I can. It's just the rest I need. You see? I can barely move. Barely talk. You can hear it, I'm sure. So, I'm going to go now. Go get that rest."

She hangs up and takes one of the headache pills, and then leans back against a mound of pillows, holding a compress soaked in warm water and apple cider vinegar across her nose. It lies over her cheekbones, loosening the mucus.

Mid-June 1962: Twentieth Century-Fox Executive Offices, Los Angeles

The brass at Twentieth Century-Fox gathers in a hastily arranged meeting. The windows closed. Shades drawn. The overhead lights are on, but the room is dim. Almost washed out. Calling in from New York, Twentieth's vice president, Peter Levathes, starts off: "We've let the inmates run the asylum." There's tentative laughter, no one quite sure what to make of that statement. But Levathes isn't laughing. Couldn't begin to tell you why anybody would find that statement funny. And for the moment he leaves it at that. Lets the idea sink in.

No one responds. They know where this heading.

Levathes speaks again, saying that, simply put, Marilyn has to be fired. *Something's Got to Give* was supposed to make up for the *Cleopatra* debacle, not add to its deficit. He's not running a charity. The film was supposed to be easy. A remake. Just update an old script and throw some stars into it. But the son of a bitch has been hijacked. How many revisions has the script gone through? How many writers? How this has gotten out of hand is obvious. Levathes says he's holding a memo. The stationery wrinkles in his fingers. "Marilyn Monroe," he recites into the telephone, "has only managed to be on set for twelve out of thirty-seven shooting days." The whole production is in a constant state of regeneration, having to readjust itself on the fly nearly every morning. And someone in the room says, "What is it with actors these days?" Levathes agrees, saying that part of it is the agents trying to muscle the contracts away from the studios. They inflate the stars into thinking they're more than they are. Pumping them up for negotiations, trying to jimmy the salaries up higher above the expense line. And Marilyn is queen of the swelled heads. The role model. At thirty-six years old in this business, she's lucky to get any leading roles, yet she acts as though she runs the motherfucking studio, shifting schedules based on her moods, and her real and imagined illnesses. It's threatening the whole system. Barely any room for a studio head anymore. She has to go. Not just for the movie, but for the sake and health of the industry.

Henry Weinstein offers a last defense. He asks, "What about what she's done for the studio? Isn't she owed some leeway or extra circumstance? There is a history here. A real history."

Levathes sighs into the phone. "The money from the world of the past," he says, "has little value in the world of the future."

Weinstein walks to the window. He pushes the curtain open with the back of his hand. Backlit, he looks like a shadow puppet. And in that moment it becomes even clearer that in Hollywood there is no past. There are trace amounts of nostalgia, just enough to keep the foundation strong. But it's a business focused on the future.

Scratch that.

A business that closes its eyes and hopes for a future.

The next day, *Los Angeles Times* gossip columnist Hedda Hopper leaks the news of Marilyn's dismissal in her column, "Hedda Hopper's Hollywood." She quotes a source who's identified only as "one of the most knowledgeable men in the industry." He's told Hopper, "I believe it is the end of her career . . . She has no control of herself." It's believed the knowledgeable man was George Cukor.

At twenty-seven, nearly ten years younger than Marilyn, Lee Remick is at her prime. Under contract with Twentieth, she is assigned to take over Marilyn's part in *Something's Got to Give*. And although the studio publicists have been trying to push her as America's answer to Brigitte Bardot, "a chick with money and breeding who's loaded with sex appeal" (something she's battled against, hiring her own publicist to push her as a serious actress who, like Marilyn, attended the Actors Studio), what makes her most suitable for this particular movie at this particular time are the qualities she described in an interview with the *New York Herald Tribune*. "My problem," she said, "is I've always been too happy. I have a lovely baby, a wonderful husband, my friends all like me, and I don't have any neuroses. I'm not an oddball. Every part I play is different because I don't bring the trademark neurosis to it . . . Why is it most actresses must be bizarre, vulgar, or temperamental to make good copy?" If Remick can really clean up in the wake of Monroe's hurricane path, Levathes is willing to call off the publicity department on the Brigitte Bardot pitch. He'll let her say she's a serious actress all she wants.

On June 8, Remick is fit and dressed in Marilyn's wardrobe, then photographed alongside George Cukor, both with reflexive smiles; a reluctant debutante and her patron. But behind the scenes she doesn't trust the motives. She suspects it's all an attempt by Twentieth Century-Fox to humiliate Marilyn Monroe. Remick asked her agent to find out if she really has to go through this, all for a measly $80,000. Additionally, time is tight—she's already obligated to a July shooting schedule for *The Running Man*. But there's no discussion. She's informed that she owes Twentieth another movie, and contrary to what her predecessor in the role might have thought, Peter Levathes is still in charge. They expect her to be gracious. Get out there and put on a good face for the sake of the picture. And to follow through with whatever the unit publicist asks for.

While she and Cukor are being paraded, Twentieth announces through its legal counsel, Musick, Peeler & Garrett, that the studio has filed a $500,000 suit against Marilyn Monroe and her company, Marilyn Monroe Productions. When contacted by a New York reporter, attorney Jesse R. O'Malley of Musick, Peeler & Garrett asserts that Marilyn Monroe is in *willful violation of contract*, and that her malfeasance has cost the studio close to $2,000,000. He predicts that when all is said and done, the suit will increase its claim of $500,000 to upward of $1,000,000. But no one talks publicly about the troubled history between Monroe and Twentieth Century-Fox, that she left them once before, in '55. Nor do they talk about the animosity, and the contracts, and the paybacks. This is about positioning. A publicity battle, designed to show Marilyn and all those who've lined up behind her who is in charge. A high-stakes bet to get the movie and the movie business back in order. It's these kinds of dealings that might bring a dose of neurosis swirling into Lee Remick's head as she marches behind the unit publicist, actually feeling like an oddball wearing someone else's costume, the material bunched and pinned behind her back so it will fit, yet smiling, using all her training to convey how honored she is to have this opportunity of a lifetime.

But then there's Dean Martin, who, upon hearing of the changes, says, Look, I have nothing against Lee Remick, but let me tell you, I signed on to work with Marilyn Monroe, and while there obviously are some issues at hand, and I know this is a business, still, it's not about the film or the script, it's about working with Marilyn, and again let me be straight here, this has nothing to do with Lee Remick, she's a fine actress, a real beauty, and I know that one day, if I never get the chance to work with her, I'll regret passing up this chance because she really is a talent, and I mean that when I say it, a real real talent, but in terms of the situation at hand, we're talking about Marilyn Monroe, and let me tell you, baby, if you don't understand what all the fuss about her is, then you only need to spend thirty seconds in her presence to find yourself hooked, and that's what doing this movie is about, that's why I signed on, for the chemistry, or at least the shot at chemistry, and again, don't get me wrong about Lee Remick, I know she's a force, I know she's an American Brigitte Bardot, I have the greatest respect for Miss Lee Remick and her talent, and all the other actresses who were considered for the role, but I signed on the dotted line to do the picture with Marilyn

Monroe and I will do it with no one else. I'll be perfectly on the money with you, lay it all out on the table, all my cards exposed: No Marilyn, no picture.

The next month keeps Marilyn busy. Doing photo shoots for magazines. *Life. Vogue. Cosmopolitan.* And for each of those pieces, she poses with a seduction that's new to her—not necessarily a sexuality that offers itself, instead one seeking to prove its vibrancy to the lens. It's as though she's trying to escape into the camera, letting it eat up the last bits of Marilyn.

On Dean Martin's insistence (and specifically because of the clause in his contract that says he'll work only with Marilyn Monroe), contract negotiations begin in order to return Marilyn to *Something's Got to Give*. For its part, Twentieth agrees to up her salary to a more commensurate level. In turn, Marilyn agrees to make two more pictures for them (without Paula Strasberg on set). For Marilyn there's one more issue. The real deal breaker. She will not work with George Cukor. Not with the way he treated her on set.

Jean Negulesco expresses interest in signing on. He directed Marilyn in *How to Marry a Millionaire*. She trusts him, believing he has true respect for actors. And she appreciates his filmmaking sensibilities, his sense for the artistry of the camera, which extends well beyond seeing the bottom line. There will be a brief hiatus to regroup and accommodate schedules, and then, assuming the terms of the new agreement can be met, they'll resume filming in October. If everything goes as planned, the lawsuit will be dropped.

Still, she can't shake Cukor's words from her head. She fired him. Brought him down. Yet he chipped away at her. Put those thoughts about her age into her head. Made it a part of her. Told her there was only one Marilyn anybody really gave a shit about, and she was flirting with losing even that.

But would it be such a bad thing to lose *that* Marilyn Monroe?

His harangues stuck. She barely trusts anyone. There are few people she can count on. Keeping balanced requires more diligence. She's gone back to doing yoga. But this time it's not about the chair or warrior postures meant to strengthen her legs; it's meant to ground her, help her find a center. And in the evenings, she's put aside *To Kill a Mockingbird* and *Franny and Zooey*, instead taking up *Autobiography of a Yogi* and the *Bhagavad Gita*.

Maybe Cukor has done her a favor? Opened the door for Marilyn Monroe to exit? She's been a good character, and had a tremendous ride. But this is not where she wants to live anymore.

At some point, when she knows she's steadied and centered, she'll thank Cukor.

When it's all over.

July 27–July 28, 1962

Cal Neva Lodge, Crystal Bay, NV

In the abstract for his article "Naked Suicide," published
in the Journal of the American Academy of Psychiatry
and the Law, *Dr. Robert Simon writes, "Nakedness during a*
suicide attempt is presumptive evidence of high risk for suicide
completion. Deliberate self-harm, without intent to die, is not
usually inflicted while naked." In the article, Simon notes that
in the case of women who have committed suicide naked, the
traditional belief has always been that it must be homicide staged
to appear as a suicide, as "'feminine modesty' carries over into
suicidal death." But this appears not to be true. In fact, it seems
that most naked suicides involve hanging or overdosing, leaving
the body ultimately exposed at its worst. The psychological
explanations for a naked suicide are up for grabs. Dr. Simon's
article suggests that some reasons may be atonement, vengeance,
or a statement of vulnerability. But for others—especially in the
case of overdoses—there may be no deliberate rationale. It's just
something that happens when you lose all sense of orientation.

11:25 PM

For a moment she forgets where she is. Where she's going. The space is musty, and it's airless, and it also smells
of men. Her stomach stings. Standing in total darkness,
she imagines that she could probably move through
this space forever without finding her way out.

It's a little like those backyard games in which
you're blindfolded and then spun. At first you might
be queasy with fear. But soon there's an inherent
trust in physics and fate, the instinctive knowledge
that you'll land facing the right direction.

Reaching out, she inadvertently strips a coat off its
hanger. It's Sinatra's jacket. She's in his closet.

Once she managed to cut out of the casino, she rushed back through the tunnel to the cottage. Going underground felt like something out of a child's fairy tale. Out of one life and into another. Holding the metal rail, she focused on each carpeted stair, measuring every step. Exposed bulbs lit the way, warm against the sweaty dampness of the walls. Midway through, she took notice of leaving the Nevada side, where the rules were not just different, they were malleable. They could be shaped. Always reinterpreted. She remembered to walk straight. *Don't take any detours.* Moving with cautious anticipation toward the exit up to Sinatra's cabin, her fingers glided along the water pipes. Men's voices followed behind, loud and urgent. Vibrating the pipes. Coming around the tunnel's elbow. Echoes of Giancana. Be vigilant, she reminded herself. Don't let them get inside you. Saying it over and over until they actually did feel inside her. Large and thorny. Forceful. Her hand jerked from the pipes, fingers folded into a fist. She turned around. Looked. Could see nothing. Then hurried onward, trying to maintain a normal pace. Never wanting to give off the scent of fear. Finally at the end of the tunnel, without ever seeing the men, she ran up the stairs and into Frank's closet, without tripping over a single step.

The moonlight off the lake radiates in through the slightly open door. And she just stands in the closet, her head next to the swinging hanger, out of range of the men in the tunnel, protected and alone.

It's like that backyard game.

She senses them coming. (*Is it Giancana and his gang? Is it Frank and his?*) Their feet bang on the cement, trampling with no pretense of delicacy. Coming to Tahoe had been about wanting to go away. Not being part of the showbiz life. But they won't let her. They'll chase her down, it seems. And, now, with the sport coat tangled around her ankles, trying to dance herself free of it, her right shoe accidentally kicks off; it flies backward, clunking against the wall.

Already she's lost time, touching every inch of the closet twice looking for the shoe. In a movie it might make for a comedic moment, a dark closet filled with bumbling gangsters and one confused, trapped blonde. But they aren't bumbling, and this isn't the pictures. Finally, she yanks off the left shoe and tosses it over her shoulder. And then makes straight for the front door. She just wants to get to her cabin. Close the door, and keep the world at bay.

The deck alongside the cabin is uneven and wobbly. Fear makes balancing nearly impossible. Their voices sound close by. She scampers up the steps; the splintered wood catches her stockings. Cabin number three is just a short distance along the walkway, but all sense of direction is skewed. Unsure of what to do, she veers right, into the swimming pool area. There the water glows, lit like an artificial opal.

Backed up into a corner. Aching feet. The nylons completely sheared on the soles. Pebbles dig into her heels. She shrinks against the corner pole of the fence surrounding the pool, hugging herself. Maybe she can disappear into the nightscape.

It does feel a little safer on the California side. There's no real explanation or tangible reason. Maybe it's the consciously promoted sense of order that contrasts with Nevada's lawless identity—its gambling, lack of speed limits, and six-week divorces. The last gasp of frontier populism. It's artificial, that California-Nevada border. An arbitrary distinction, designated through deals and compromises and left to a cartographer's hand to show. But somehow the border does feel real. A physical object. Like a fortress, protecting a way of life. Or keeping one out. Depending on how you look at it.

Across the street, as clouds start to gather, a moon shadow caps the west side of the hill. The bodyguard was wrong. You can see it from here, if you're positioned just right. Maybe it's about how the earth tilts. Halfway down there's a movement. Joe is standing in a small open space between two pines. One of the last beams of moonlight highlights him. And though he is tiny, a pinprick in the distance, there's no question. She'd know the posture anywhere. The way his hands sit on his hips when he's disappointed. How his feet shift in place when he feels helpless. She lifts her hand and gives a subtle wave, just a slight wiggle, four fingers.

The shadow keeps moving down the hill. A slow slide toward him.

Nevada once felt right. It certainly did when Arthur went there in 1956 for his divorce, in order to marry her. He just needed a resident witness affidavit, stating he'd been seen living in the state for the requisite month and a half. And there were so many Nevadans willing to vouch for Arthur. It seemed as though the entire Silver State were cheering him on, like a collective best man for his wedding. It made her glad to return to Nevada to film *The Misfits*. As though she owed the state something. How quickly she learned to dread it. The alkali flats of Pyramid Lake. Endless drives to Dayton and the waiting in the brutal heat. The mornings and evenings spent at the Mapes Hotel in Reno, where each day she found it more and more impossible to be in the same space as her husband of barely four years, a physical reaction that even she knew lacked logic or merit. Six weeks was all it took. Now, four and a half years later, she'd gladly stay on the California side forever.

There's that magic trick sometimes called the Sword Cabinet, or the Sword Through Box, where the assistant, typically a scantily clad woman, lies inside a box on a table. The magician takes sword after sword, jabbing them into the box at every conceivable angle. All along the sides. Sometimes from the bottom. Sometimes from the top. Every angle. To heighten the illusion, the magician will pull a selection of men out of the audience, inviting them up on stage, also to stab the woman in the box. Sword after sword after sword. At the end, when the brands are removed and the box is opened, the woman is revealed to be unharmed. But even the best magicians know there's a calculated risk to doing this nightly. One can't just keep giving men swords and expect that not even one will eventually hit.

She can't see the men, but they have to be there. They must be on Sinatra's porch, leaning against the railing, puffing cigarettes and watching smoke rings mist out toward the lake. She feels cornered. While another's survival instincts might take over, she only cowers, pushing herself harder against the steel fence post, as though fusing it with her spine.

Just above the pool area, she can see the Circle Bar. It's crowded, and loud. The spillover following Frank's invitation from the stage for a drink. Pat's probably pushing her way through it, trying to get to Frank to make her case. Some people gather in front of the window. A woman is making a point, her palm turned up, unaware her martini glass is emptying. It doesn't seem fair to hear lilting, careless chatter as though there are no dangers in the world.

The swimming pool is the epitome of the Cal Neva's location. Not quite kidney-shaped, its stand-out feature is the tiled black line that splits the pool, with each side marked appropriately, *California* and *Nevada*. However, it's not divided down the middle, as some people think. The California portion makes up only about a third of the pool. The shallow end.

And she pictures herself as any one of those women she grew up seeing in Norwalk State Hospital. Always a half step off the beat, yet moving with a sense of assurance. But when met by the rest of the world, they turned afraid, went inward. Like a peaceable tribe confronted by its aggressor.

Up the hill, the shadow moves faster, a slow avalanche. She can still see Joe, and she doesn't know if he's there to protect her or just to shake his head in disappointment and shame. The hill keeps getting darker. She can barely make him out. Why is he letting the moon shadow wash over him? Can't he tell? She raises her hands, trying to signal him, mouthing, *Move down. Move down. I need you.*

To protect themselves from predators, some insects rely on hiding, camouflaging themselves within their habitat, heads down and bodies still, counting on not being seen. Others, however, protect themselves through mimicry, evolving in a way that allows them to take on the characteristics of their predators. The insect survives because the hunter often will move right past its prey, unaware it sees anything other than its own kind.

With Joe finally lost in darkness, she pushes herself away from the pole and walks out of the pool area in a slow shuffle, one foot barely in front of the other, scraping out a rhythm that seems familiar, her limbs heavier, her hair more tousled, and the gravel boring into her feet. She's sure she hears gruff voices bellowing off Sinatra's porch, unaware, and seemingly uncaring, that she's anywhere near.

There is no safety. Booby traps are around every corner. But they're without identifiable form, only the abstract shapes of a publicized lawsuit or a series of unseen threats or a lifesaving plan gone wrong. All she can do is go back to her cabin, polish off the warm champagne left on top of the wicker desk, light a candle and take some pills, spread out on her bed, and hide under the protection of night.

11:50 PM

Frank opens her door without knocking, dangling her shoes like a keepsake. The black heels swing past each other, clacking. He's still dressed in the clothes from his show—slim black pants, a white button-down, and a matching coat. Only the fedora has been left behind.

272

He looks a little shiny all over, his eyes watering and his skin gleaming in the glow of a candle she's lit. Running a hand through his hair, swaying, he looks down at her in the bed. He pinches the edge of a poppy plant in the water-glass bouquet. The petal falls off and to the floor. He kicks it toward the bed.

She's on her back atop the comforter. Still dressed. Bare feet. The flame from the nearly burnt-out candle reflects on her face. Champagne bottles lie on their sides on the floor; the pill containers are lined along the desk, two opened, their white lids missing. Looking at him she says, "Frank," then closes her eyes with a half smile.

He sits at the end of the bed, placing the shoes beside him. His knees point outward. Taking hold of her left ankle, he slowly lifts her foot up onto his lap. He slips the corresponding shoe onto her foot. "At last I've found my princess," he says. "And boy did she do a number on my closet."

She says nothing.

Frank scoots up the bed. He stops only to smooth the wrinkles from his pants. Her other shoe falls to the floor, landing on its side. He folds a pillow under his neck, then puts an arm around her. "I'd at least figured on you joining me for a drink after the show," he says, wiggling beside her. "Was I that bad?"

"You, Frank, were wonderful. As always."

"Then what gives? Why did you let me down?"

And she wants to talk, but she can hardly speak more than a few words at a time before her mind shifts and forgets where it's going. Anger is churning inside, and she's not even sure what it's directed at, other than that she can't stop being in a world she doesn't want to be in. What she does manage to tell Frank is that she came into this weekend planning to go up, up, up, but that the things he claimed wouldn't be there *were* there, and they snared her when no one was looking, and now she's going down, down, down. And he says, "Things *I* claimed? *When no one was looking*? What the hell are you talking about?" And she says, "Not your show, Frank. Your wonderful show. Time should've stopped there." And he sits upright, wresting his arm back from around her neck, the pillow tumbling to the floor.

"Now don't get loony on me," he says.

And that makes her smile. *Loony*. His crisp Jersey accent almost makes it sound charming.

How quickly he can turn. Through his clenched jaw his voice sounds on edge. "You just have no idea what a mess you are, do you?"

"No." She shakes her head. Then she nods. "Well, sort of."

He tells her she best snap out of it quick, because if she's like this tomorrow, then he's shipping her back, and she can take that yapping Pat Lawford with her. He's not running a halfway house for mental breakdowns, he says. This is a place to relax and enjoy yourself, no matter who you are. For *all* his friends. A community. "Morning," he declares. "Figure it out by morning. Figure out how the Marilyn I invited can be back here and present." He leans over and blows out the candle. It seems only her face has gone dark, like a reverse spotlight. And then he exits the room, leaving it almost as it was when he came in, except that she has one shoe on her foot, the other on the floor, the bouquet is slightly more wilted, and the candle is snuffed out.

"Morning," he calls back through the closed door.

"Morning," she whispers. And as she hears his steps pound off the porch, she rolls over onto her side and hugs a pillow, chanting to herself, "Tomorrow is tomorrow is tomorrow is tomorrow."

With Frank gone, the main objective is to sleep. "Snap out of it" by morning. Sometimes the yellow warning sign tells her not to stand too close to the edge. Other times it tells her to beware of falling rocks. That's why the doctors and nurses give out pills. To help avoid that step that will put you in harm's way. A security barrier away from the edge and a protective umbrella against any falling rocks. *It's a matter of safety.* Didn't the nurses at Norwalk often say that to her almost apologetically, after forcing a regimen of pills on her mother?

* *Decadron phosphate*
* *Chloral hydrate*
* *Rx 80521*
* *Rx 80522*

* *Rx 13525*
* *Rx 13526*
* *Seconal*

No one has ever been able to tell her which are the best meds for her. Dr. Engleberg has barely even entertained the question when she's asked. He's told her she's in over her head, and she says, "I just think you're trying to control me," and he laughs and says, "You always make me laugh. No matter what." And she says, "No, really," but he cuts her off, "No, really. When you get a medical degree, then we can have the debate." "Now," she says, "you're making me laugh." It's a regular conversation, one that always ends with her false acquiescence. They both know she keeps other kinds of downers, a stash that's picked up regularly for her in Tijuana. It's just a matter of trying to remember which is which. She can never keep the colors straight.

She pushes a strand of hair behind her ear, then drops down a mystery pill (Rx 13525), chasing it with champagne.

Here's to *snapping out of it.*

12:11 AM

The zipper on her dress is undone. She's on her stomach, propped up by an elbow. The sconces are dimmed, with just a trace of moonlight seeping through the blinds. A thin sheet of air blows over her back, the exposed skin chilled and goose-bumped. The telephone line stretches to the center of the bed, barely making it past the mound of pillows—a taut string vibrating just above the sheets.

She dials out of instinct. It's probably the booze and her nerves, but the ringing sounds like a series of infinite spirals, a mechanical purr that abruptly stops with *hello*. She recognizes the voice, almost as familiar as her own. She can't place it, though she can connect it to the Actors Studio. It's as though her short-term-memory fuse has blown. "Who is this?" Marilyn asks.

"You're the one who called."

"I know I called. But . . ."

"Jeannie," the voice answers suspiciously.

"Jeannie who?"

"Is that you, Marilyn?"

"Do you mean Jeannie Carmen?"

"Jesus, Marilyn. It's Jeannie."

"What are you doing now, Jeannie?" Marilyn says, her voice deepening a little. It doesn't sound like Jeannie.

"It's not a good time . . . You know what I mean . . . ? Not a good time to . . . You know what I mean, right? And aren't you in Lake Tahoe? That's what someone said."

She doesn't say anything. She takes her glass off the nightstand and sips the last of the champagne.

"Marilyn . . . ? Still there, Marilyn?"

"Yes. Marilyn's still here."

"Sweetheart, can we talk in the morning? Is that all right?"

"I'm just so tired, Jeannie. Can't get to sleep. Almost *too* tired to get to sleep, if that's possible . . . You see, I just can't tell these pills apart, and the labels don't mean anything . . . Nothing here makes sense, and I'm just wondering if you'd be able to tell . . .?"

Jeannie laughs. It almost steams out of the phone. "Look, I can barely . . ."

"But let me describe them."

"Marilyn, it's the middle of the night. And it sounds as though maybe you've already had enough. Know what I mean? I'm a little bit, you know . . . Plus I've got a small crowd here, and, on top of that, it's kind of hard to hear."

"I can tell you the colors, maybe. Try to say them loud and quick. I just want to find the right one is all. I'm just so exhausted. And I want to find the right one that'll work."

Jeannie's breathing is suddenly really loud. Men and women break into laughter behind her. It sounds so far away through the receiver. Again, Jeannie asks, "Marilyn? Listen. I want you to put yourself to sleep right quick, and do it without any pills, and then come morning you can let Norma Jeane come out to play. Put the floozy to bed, and get out the horn-rims, and bring out all of Norma Jeane's talk-talk-talk, like we're in New York again, where the smarts are, and where all the rest of those LA shits can go to . . . You know what I'm saying. Marilyn needs to go to sleep now. Send out Norma Jeane."

"Jeannie, if you could help me tell them apart, is all."

"Honey, it would take me a week alone just to unravel the phone cord. I'm in no shape, my dear, to match colors long distance. Tonight is not the night. Just let yourself fall asleep now."

"Please, Jeannie."

"Oh, Nor-ma," she calls into the phone with a prairie cadence. "Nor-ma Jeane. Come out, come out, wherever you are."

12:25 AM

The phone in cabin three has been off the hook for an unusually long time. The hotel operator notices it while plugging a line in through the manual exchange—a little glowing jack, flickering like a pesky insect. She has the feeling it's been there for a while; she just didn't pay attention while taking so many calls throughout the evening. It's a feeling. She knows it's not her job to judge or to presume what goes on in the guests' rooms, but her instinct tells her to let someone know that she thinks something is wrong. It's a professional ethic. One that trumps matters of privacy.

12:40 AM

Passing clouds partially eclipse the moon. The light in the cabin further fades. She just wants to go to sleep. She reaches out over the edge of the bed and grips the first bottle she touches. It's like Braille. She fingers out a single capsule. It might be blue. It could be green. She holds the capsule above her mouth and pricks a small hole in the end of it with a safety pin. Sticking out her tongue in slow motion, she catches the falling powder, swallows, and feels it mix with her bloodstream. She stretches her arms over her head and drops the spent capsule behind the headboard. Empty and clear, it will blend into the green carpet.

12:48 AM

The hotel operator notifies the management about the unusual amount of time the phone has been off the hook in cabin three. They call Mr. Sinatra. He swears, then says it isn't his problem either, he's done intervening with her for the night. He has no time for this kind of crap. But then he calms. Thinks on it. A decision's made to send Peter Lawford to her cabin; he can just give a polite rap on the door, poke his head inside to make sure everything's okay. She trusts him, Sinatra says. It's a Hollywood understanding. Who knows? Maybe she'll be sitting on the bed, the phone crooked between her neck and shoulders waving him off or signaling *just a moment.* Or she could be asleep, unaware that when she kicked off her shoe, the heel knocked the receiver over, and she'd drifted off without noticing the pulsing tone.

The operator hopes it will be something more. In some respects she's put her job on the line by sounding the alarm. It's serious business to risk the privacy of the guests—especially ones who are promised seclusion. The operator's moral side hopes the phone being off the hook has a simple, innocuous explanation. But in the most private corner of her mind, she holds out for something just horrible enough to give her alarm justification.

1:03 AM

She can barely see straight anymore, and though she's flat on the bed, she's balled up, feeling herself in free flight, sinking down. She's still fully clothed but her evening dress seems to hover above her, humming like some sort of electric coating. Her palms push flat against the mattress to break the fall. She slows a little. Once it's finally safe to let go of the bed, she'll work her body out of the dress and kick the garment off, where it will slump to the floor. Then she'll stretch out across the bed, fully nude and no longer constricted. And then just be. She lets up slightly on her grip, only to plunge further.

1:20 AM

She barely notices him when he bursts through the door.

Her right leg sticks out of the covers, twitching, her foot on the verge of cramping, the toes and the arch contracting. What's left of the moonlight flows down her thighs, and she swears she can feel it running off her ankles, puddling on the sheets. Her left hand is clenched into a fist. The right holds on to the telephone receiver, cradled against her hip. She glances up, barely able to see straight. Trying to look is like staring into an eclipse.

He stands too large for the room. Pulling at his fingers. The joints popping in little bursts of thunder. Stepping forward, he accidentally kicks a champagne bottle. It rolls under the bed and knocks against a leg. A dull chime.

"Hi," she says. Her gums stick together, her mouth dry. She drops the phone. It dangles off the bed.

He lets out a sigh, as though relieved to know she's alive.

Could she look that dead?

Before she knows it his thumbs hook under her armpits. He pulls her up until she's propped against the headboard. She can feel his breath blowing warm down her back. For his own sake, he tugs the bedsheets up to cover her breasts. "Marilyn," he finally says. "Can you hear me? I know you're in there, Marilyn."

His voice is not just directed at her. It's surrounding her, pouring in at all the unsuspecting places.

She nods her head in affirmation. But it must not look like much, because he keeps asking if she can hear him. All the while lightly slapping her cheek.

She feels herself sinking again. Being drawn back down into the bed.

Suddenly, water is falling over her, head and torso, slowly bringing her back up to the surface.

She nods. Feels her body. Touches her hips. No longer sinking.

With her eyes beginning to focus, it looks as if it's Peter Lawford shaking out the last of the ice bucket over her head. Not Joe? It isn't that she's had a real reason to believe it'd be Joe. She just sort of expected it would be.

11:10 AM

By late morning the sheets have dried. One stream of light comes between the curtains. The room is already warm. She's slept through breakfast.

Initially she rolls out of bed as though it's any other day, stretching her legs and arms and rolling her neck. Her fingers splay toward the ceiling, elongating her spine. Her hips pop, as though they've been jammed into their sockets too tightly. And then she sees the room, and she smells the stale stink of last night, which brings everything back, reminding her that her head is throbbing and that her eyeballs might burst.

The physical remnants that the disaster left behind:

* The ice bucket on the floor
* Pill bottles turned over on every surface
* A wilted bouquet of wildflowers
* The nub of the candle tilted and lying in a puddle of its own wax
* Bottles and glasses

She walks right to the mirror arched over the bureau, places her sticky palms flat on the dresser top, and leans in to the mirror until her face nearly touches the surface. Her hair is stringy and matted, her eyes puffed, and her skin almost pure white. She huffs a breath against the glass, looking for a billow of fog, just to make sure she's still alive.

She doesn't know what will be waiting outside the door, or who will be there, or where the escape holes are.

She slips on a pair of capris, her green Pucci top, and unballs a scarf, tying it over her head. She feels like a primitive in a mask with bug eyes and exaggerated features, meant to ward off marauding sprits and enemies.

This is what failure looks like. How it lives. Like a room on a ward, where your disappointments and fears live among you as taunting reminders, while out-side there's a world that's festively alive, but which you can't enter because your disappointments and fears won't let you out.

12:00 PM

Coming in for her afternoon shift, the hotel operator re-turns to the front desk. The first thing she does is check the switchboard, to confirm that the line for cabin three is properly hung up. And even if it weren't she wouldn't say anything. There's been no word about what actu-ally happened in the middle of the night. Whether her alarm was warranted. Nobody's whispered any rumors. There've been no leaked details. In fact, she knows that if she pushes a little for information, needles some of her coworkers with vague hints and leading questions, they won't reply because they won't know what she's talking about. Which is precisely why she won't say anything again, if placed in a similar circumstance.

She understands the shape of privacy.

12:07 PM

On the landing below her cabin's deck, she spots Sina-tra and Buddy Greco. They're bordered by a giant rock wedged in the mountainside and the tall pines that cascade down to the lakeshore. Sinatra, in his swim trunks, lounges shirtless in a deck chair, reading the paper, his bony shoulders streaked by sunlight, bare legs crossed. Wearing a khaki jungle-style short-sleeved shirt with matching trousers, Greco is getting a haircut. He keeps looking around the grounds, and the barber jerks his head back in place, annoyed at the interruption of his snipping.

She waves to Frank; he's been the one solid thing for her.

Peering over the top of his newspaper, Sinatra catches her eye. "So the queen's come out of her chamber," he announces. The paper drops into his lap. A page slips off, and the wind skirts it across the concrete. He shakes his head: "The definition of a civilization in ruins." He motions her away. A brushstroke.

She stays put. Adjusts her sunglasses. On her face they feel like part of a villain's disguise. "Frank?" she starts with a weak voice.

The wind blows the paper in a circle around the landing, until it comes back, wrapped against his ankle. He kicks the sheet away. "Can it," he says. "Pack your bags, and go home." He snaps his fingers, disappearing her.

And with that snap she's invisible. She grips on to the safety rail to keep from falling down. All she can imagine doing is bounding down the stairs, heading toward the lake, building her velocity, in hopes that she might sail across Lake Tahoe and just fade away.

Postscript

One Week Later

Covering Marilyn Monroe's death, the August 6, 1962, edition of the Los Angeles Times *reported, "Coroner Theodore J. Curphey today ordered a 'psychiatric autopsy' for Marilyn Monroe." The psychiatric autopsy, sometimes called the psychological autopsy, was introduced and refined by Drs. Edwin Shneidman, Norman Farberow, and Robert Litman of the Suicide Prevention Center at Los Angeles County General Hospital. Their method relied on a series of interviews with friends and colleagues of the deceased— essentially a conversational gathering of evidence to develop a postmortem psychological history. While it could point to various causes of death, its marquee objective was to determine if there had been a suicide. From a clinical research standpoint it was also hoped the practice would provide critical information for suicide prevention. Monroe's psychological autopsy report was never made public. At one point it was leaked that one of the study's conclusions described her as having a "suicidal state of mind prior to her death." But that didn't make it to the papers. It was hardly news.*

As a footnote, nearly all articles about the practice of psychiatric autopsies credit Marilyn Monroe for bringing the practice to national attention.

Upon her death, Peter Levathes was quoted in the papers as saying that the studio's lawsuit would not be "pressed against her estate."

The August 6 New York Times *article about her death painted Marilyn as being, by the end, a "virtual recluse."*

Her bedroom was described as "sparse." Just a bed. A dressing table. An end table. And a telephone from the hallway, its cord stretched across the mussed sheets.

August 7, 1962:
Westwood Village Mortuary, Los Angeles

Three days straight it took.

Nothing but quiet.

At the Westwood Village Mortuary a few family members mingled among the staff. A makeup man and a wardrobe woman waited, on call for the eventual dressing. But other than that, no Hollywood types. Joe DiMaggio had made sure of that. Muttered under his breath that they were the ones who did this to her. Muttered a lot of things under his breath, without saying much of anything to anybody. He kept his reserve, instead charging Allan Abbott of Abbott and Hast Funeral Services to oversee the details for the service and its preparations, instructing him to hire and post six Pinkerton guards to keep the showbiz people out, with additional orders to prevent postmortem photographs, as well as be sure nothing was snipped from the body as a souvenir. It was quiet in the mortuary. Quiet, except for the embalmer at work. And the squeaking soles of the six Pinkerton guards.

On the third day, something doesn't look right. They're getting ready to dress her, but the embalmer won't leave the table. She looks swollen. Her neck is bulging like a bodybuilder's, puffed out as though it could burst. The embalmer steps back. "Do you see it?" he asks Mary, one of the mortuary's co-owners. Then he looks over at Abbott, who can only shrug. The embalmer doesn't talk much. He prefers not to say things that don't need to be said. At one time the embalmer wished he were deaf, until he realized it wasn't noise on its own that bothered him, just unnecessary noise. People are surprised when he speaks. Almost honored. "I'm not imagining it, Mary, am I?"

"You're not."

"Then you see it too?" He squints his eyes, head cocked.

"You're not."

"Meaning, I don't see it?"

"Meaning, no. You're not imagining it, is what I mean to say. You're not, is what I'm saying."

He pokes at the neck with the blunt end of a scalpel, trying to measure the density. Seeing how firm her neck is. Then he touches it with his index finger, pushing in slightly, feeling through the latex that it's all fluid; something inside has weakened, causing the embalming chemicals to leak internally. A reservoir in her neck.

The embalmer steps back and reconsiders. He pinches the bridge of his nose, then shakes his head in some disappointment. It's only that he'd thought he was done, is all. If the embalmer were married, he'd have to call home to tell his wife he'd be late for dinner. And though he'd work carefully into the night, going through the extra steps to remedy and reconstruct, somehow the embalmer knows he'd be fighting the urge to rush. But he has the whole evening. He circles her body, trying to find the best way in for the incision.

"I don't think we can leave her this way," Mary says.

"No."

"You mean she may have to stay this way?"

The embalmer picks up the scalpel and runs it across his smock. Not really sharpening it. Not quite cleaning it. He thinks that action must answer the question. To explain any more would only be noise.

He takes a pair of scissors to her hair, trimming around the back, so he can get at the least visible part of the neck. Her hair is coarse and strawlike. Not much different from a doll's. The studio technicians gasp at the sound of the chopping scissors. It must seem like defiling to them. Abbott scurries over quickly with a broom and dustpan, trying to be useful. The hair is dumped into a barrel along with all the wadded papers, gauze, and leftover suture clippings.

Mary says it looks as though this might take some time, and she promised Mr. DiMaggio an update. Abbott thinks that is a good idea, as Mr. DiMaggio wants to be kept abreast of all the steps. He doesn't want anybody trying to take anything over. She nods in agreement, saying she'll be back shortly, unless the embalmer needs her help.

The embalmer doesn't reply. He's bent over, his back to the door, twisting the head slowly in the support, for access. He focuses as though lining up his shot, then he's incising the scalpel into the back of her neck. He cuts a little to both sides, letting the fluid drain into a pan. Though this procedure was unexpected, it's not far from the routine. One of a series of variables. When he's finished he'll suture the incision, then step back to observe the dressing, ensuring there are no more surprises. Then he'll go home. It's been a long three days.

"Okay," he says to the studio people. "Ready."

"We can? It's okay to . . . ?"

"Ready."

The two studio people walk up to the table. Abbott moves with them slowly. He's just going to observe. Oversee.

The embalmer does his best to stay out of their way, standing off to the side, implying that he'll help lift her body when needed. It shouldn't be a big deal to put a dress on her. The embalmer doesn't like fussing. He's lived alone most of his adult life, not because he is incapable of being with someone, but more because of what he has observed: a relationship, especially marriage, seems to be ritualized fussing.

The dress is pale green. It was sewn in Italy. The dresser has mentioned that several times, maybe his way of saying she's being buried with the class she's earned. The dresser smoothes the material with his hand over and over, almost stroking it. And he keeps trying to spit out words, until eventually he says *this can't be so*, and his chest starts to heave like he's either going to throw up or burst into tears. He turns his head to protect the dress. The embalmer looks away because he doesn't want any part of this. Of course the embalmer knows how significant this particular death is, but still he expects professionals to act as such, no matter how meaningful some people seem to find her. He saw *The Misfits* last year (although more for Gable), and it was the first time he'd seen her in a movie. She wasn't as dopey and light as he'd imagined, based on how she'd been portrayed in the papers, and her acting wasn't half bad; for the most part he believed her as Roslyn, and not as a starlet. He felt a little for Roslyn's loneliness, but not like he did for Gable's character, Gay—a solitary man in a world that will no longer allow for solitary men. And when he heard the news of her death—and nobody should mince words: *suicide*—he thought to himself, *Well, I guess she wasn't that light.* But that was a person, and this is a body—with cotton stuffed under its eyelids, and disinfectant sprayed up the nose and in the rear, and the organs full of preservatives. The only thing that gets to the embalmer is the Yankee Clipper. The thought of meeting DiMaggio makes him a little weak. He knows he'll want to say something, but he doesn't know what, other than that it will probably be the wrong thing.

Mary is back in the room, watching the dresser pull down the hem for the last time, smoothing the last wrinkle. She stands back with her arms crossed. The embalmer knows that something is wrong. He's seen this expression on her before—cheeks sucked in, eyes half narrowed somewhere between horror and exhaustion. It's tied to her need for perfection. He looks at the body, trying to decipher what's being seen through Mary's eyes. The neck appears normal again. The body's positioned in the appropriate fashion. The dress fits nicely; the lines are even and properly adjusted. But Mary is breathing louder through her nose. Her face gone flush. Finally she says, "This isn't right." Her voice is calm and modulated, but the embalmer can tell the force behind it. "No, not right."

He thinks to ask her what is not right, but he's not sure he wants to initiate a dialogue. Perhaps it will just be something that she needed to say, and that will end it. Mary is under a lot of pressure with this one. Between the media, the studio, the family, and DiMaggio, it's all pushing in on her. Maybe she just needs to let some of it off.

"Is it something with the dress?" the dresser asks. His expression is one of embarrassment and offense. "Because if it's the dress, I can . . ."

"It's not the dress."

The embalmer wishes she would just say what it *is*, not what it *isn't*. But he holds back from telling that to Mary, not wanting to get involved with the fuss.

"She looks like a man," Mary speaks just above a whisper. "See her chest. Flat as a boy's." Now she's looking right at the embalmer. "Flat as a twelve-year-old boy."

"It's from the procedure," he begins to explain. "The embalming process causes the . . . The tissues start to . . . I used some breast enhancers to—the family brought them in . . . It compensated some, but I suppose . . . Well, then, I suppose you don't think so." And it's not that he can't explain it, he just can't grasp the words, especially under Mary's focused stare.

"I can't send her out like this," Mary says. "Not in front of Mr. DiMaggio. Or her family."

What he feels like saying is: What does it really matter? He knows that when a woman lies down her breasts flatten a little, that's no secret, and laid out and dressed, she looks perfectly appropriate given the circumstance and the position. To puff her up, to enhance her to unnatural proportions while supine, would make her appear almost superhuman, even more unrealistic than she looked on the movie screen. They keep forgetting she's just a body now. Maybe it's that Mary and Abbott are driven by the need to justify everything to Mr. DiMaggio, but if the embalmer saw DiMaggio, and was the type who could speak frankly with him, he'd tell him that very thing: she's a body now. And tell him he should feel no shame for knowing that.

"I just need a minute to think," Mary says, pacing. "Ideas? Allan?" Then she looks to the studio people. "Anybody?" But they're too stunned to answer. Instead they make as though they're thinking, and their expressions, the embalmer sees, look like the smell of sweat. They're not like Mary or Abbott. They don't have to buy into this myth; they are part of it.

She is walking in circles. Drumming her fingers along her thighs. Then over to the body, where she turns to the dresser and tells him to help her open the dress. He looks at her, stunned in place, and she says that in case he didn't hear her she needs help getting the dress opened, that she needs access to the body, and she doesn't want to tear the dress of Italian origin, but she'd be willing to if necessary, because this is that important.

With the dress loosened at the top, Mary reaches under and pulls out the falsies, one at a time. "Put these somewhere safe, in case the family wants them back," she instructs no one in particular, handing them to Abbott. Then she goes over to the supply cabinet and

pulls down all the available cotton, telling the embalmer he'll need to order more, as she's about to use up his
whole inventory.

The embalmer watches Mary reach her hands under the dress, and the sight sends a quick shock along
his thigh that he feels a little embarrassed about; and
he watches the bosom slowly rise with each of Mary's
handfuls of cotton, as she says more than once, "Now
that looks like Marilyn Monroe." And he thinks he
might have been wrong. It does not look so freakish;
in fact it makes her look strangely more lifelike, and he
thinks of DiMaggio, and he thinks of DiMaggio looking at the body, and how DiMaggio must have seen her
every way from Sunday, at her best and her worst, but
more than likely the majority of time at her average,
and how when DiMaggio looks down at her for the last
time, he will see her as she was created by the studios,
further enhanced by the hands of an anxious mortuary
owner; and when DiMaggio looks down at her, hating the business of Hollywood, hating every thought
and belief that they put into her head, believing that
their success was her poison, all the while keeping his
mouth shut but in his mind accusing them of murder,
when he looks down at her, at this final creation, the
embalmer can't help but suspect that this version of
her actually is the one Mr. DiMaggio wants to remember, and that has got to be a killer because it means he,
Joe DiMaggio, is a part of it too.

Acknowledgments

Misfit is a work of fiction, primarily meant to examine a struggle for identity in a very public world, and the rewards and pitfalls of conforming to meet others' expectations. Therefore, despite many of the principal characters having the names of actual people, their thoughts, actions, and motivations are of the author's imagination. *Misfit* should not be read as a biography, or as a record of actual events. Still, there were numerous sources that helped give context to the world of the novel, and helped to frame many of the events that take place in the book:

The archives of the *New York Times, Los Angeles Times, Los Angeles Mirror-News, San Francisco Chronicle, San Francisco Examiner, Life, Confidential,* and *Time,* and other magazines of the era. Also helpful were "Naked Suicide" by Robert I. Simon, MD (*Journal of the American Academy of Psychiatry and the Law*) and "The Father of Scandal" by Victor Davis (*British Journalism Review*); *The Misfits* by Serge Toubiana, *My Story* by Marilyn Monroe and Ben Hecht, *The Story of the Misfits* by James Goode, *After the Fall* by Arthur Miller, *The Misfits* by Arthur Miller, *Timebends: A Life* by Arthur Miller, *A Method to Their Madness: The History of the Actors Studio* by Foster Hirsch, *A Player's Place: The Story of the Actors Studio* by David Garfield, and *The Road to Reno* by Inge Morath; many DVD documentaries were helpful for capturing the essence of the time; people I spoke with included Ginny Blasgen, Carolyn Foland, Amy Henderson, Cynthia Langhof, the staff of the Los Angeles County Records Center, the staff of the Van Nuys Airport Guide, and the staff of the San Francisco Public Library; innumerable websites that were critical for locating various pieces of minutiae; the FBI files on Monroe, Arthur Miller, and Sam Giancana—hundreds of pages that not only provided specific details but also spoke loudly to the perceptions of the era; and also necessary to mention is the staff at the Cal Neva Lodge who gave me detailed tours and answered more questions than anybody should have to, helping this "story" come to life for me.

Lastly, the following thanks are in order for the ways in which they contributed to this book actually seeing the light of day: Robert Boyers, Edward J. Delaney, Michael

Gizzi, Phillip Lopate, Bill Ratner, and Steve Yarbrough; Nat Sobel and Judith Weber, and everybody in their office who read too many versions of this; the unbelievable group at Tin House who know that getting it right is the first priority (Lee Montgomery, Win McCormack, Tony Perez, Nanci McCloskey, Rob Spillman, and the indispensably indispensable Meg Storey); and finally to my friends and family, who contribute in ways they don't even know.